CAPTAIN ZERO:
THE MARK OF ZERO!

THE MARK OF ZERO!

By G.T. Fleming-Roberts

STEEGER BOOKS • 2020

PUBLISHING HISTORY

"The Mark of Zero!" originally appeared in the January 1950 (Vol. 1, No. 2) issue of *Captain Zero* magazine. Copyright © 1950 by Popular Publications, Inc. Copyright renewed © 1978 and assigned to Steeger Properties, LLC. All rights reserved.

CHAPTER 1
V FOR VIOLENCE

I T WAS, Henshaw reflected, like finding a face in the figured grain of the wood that paneled his uncle's library. You saw it out of the corners of your eyes, and then when you looked at it directly, it was gone. But you kept looking until you found it again, and then it held you.

The ugliness of the man's face held you.

Henshaw found it now over the rim of his upraised glass, across the low-ceilinged basement room, in the corner there behind a small table with a red-and-white checkered cloth. A narrow face, pale in the half-light within the dive, faintly mottled like blue cheese, with a wisp of cigarette smoke trailing across it.

Evil personified, Henshaw thought. A bad man in a bad movie. Send over one Villain with a capital V for a face. V for Violence. In spite of the heat trapped within the room, a chill twisted Henshaw's shoulders. He let the face slip away in the kaleidoscopic pattern of shadows dancing to juke box rhythm, glanced at the girl beside him, and then down at the group of snapshots she had taken from her purse.

"Here's the houseboat, and here's the Wabash from Second Island. And here's—me." A slight embarrassed pause before she showed him a picture of herself in a bathing suit. "Would you like that, Artie?" she asked timidly.

"Sure," Henshaw said. "It must be fun. The ol' Wabash. The

1

shick—sycamores." That was a hell of a word when you were half tooted.

"I mean the picture. Me."

He looked at her curiously. Whenever he opened his sample cases in Pendleville, he knew he could count on Hattie McClaren for an evening. She was fun, and he took his fun where he found it. But she wasn't beautiful, as Maria was beautiful.

Something of the soft prettiness of youth remained to Hattie.

Lee Allyn came hurtling down
the sidewalk just as Dawson
fired the fifth shot.

To a marked degree she seemed to have escaped the tarnish of Pendleville's notorious Canal Street. The neckline of her sleazy dress had slipped off one shoulder, and her flesh had a warm, golden cast. Her face was heart-shaped, cute and boneless, her dark and pretty hair fluffed out in a short bob.

"Sure, Hattie," he replied belatedly and slipped the picture into his wallet. "I'll keep it next to my heart."

He saw her wince and immediately regretted that he had spoken lightly. For the first time he felt oddly uneasy in her presence and tried to escape the sensation by lighting a cigarette. Through the first wisp of smoke he saw the face of evil again. That pallid triangle. Those narrow, malevolent eyes watching from the dark corner.

When he had first noticed the face, Henshaw had accepted its owner as a part of the atmosphere of any hide-away that catered to after-hours liquor traffic. Now it seemed something more important than that, as though the place itself was evil and the man in the corner was a definite and permanent part of it. This wasn't the sort of a place for Hattie, Henshaw decided. He ought to get her out of here.

Henshaw put his lighter down on the table. Beside him, the girl was quiet, downcast.

"Look, let's have fun," Henshaw said with a show of gaiety. Let's have 'nother li'l drink, then—"

She glanced up quickly. "Oh, Artie, should you? I mean, if it was Saturday night. But you said you had to be on your toes tomorrow. Some important customers, and your uncle was anxious you should get their accounts. Maybe if we just finish what we have here, that'll be enough. Huh, Artie?"

HE DIDN'T say anything. His eyes locked with hers. He couldn't remember that anyone had looked at him in just that way in a long time—eyes soft with concern. On impulse, he put his hand under the table and found hers, small and warm and instantly responsive to his touch. Her smile was real and a trifle sad. Her eyes were misty.

For a second they were completely alone in the crowded room. That tiny dot of time was theirs. And then a dancing couple swayed aside, and the narrow wedge of face intruded from its corner. And Henshaw thought, I've got to get out of here. I've got to get *her* out of here. Whatever she is, she doesn't belong in a spot like this.

He said, "Who's that, Hattie? Keeps staring at us. Guy with the white face, alone at the corner table."

The girl's eyes searched through the murk. Her body stiffened perceptibly. Her rouged lips fell apart.

"I—I don't know," she stammered. "One of the characters, I guess." She uttered a short laugh and, with a sudden flurry of motion, swept the snapshots from the table and into her purse. " 'Scuse me, Artie, will you?"

He nodded. She stood slowly, her eyes still on his face. One long, reluctant look before she turned and slipped off somewhere beyond the shadowy couples on the dance floor.

Henshaw presumed she'd gone to the powder room. And as soon as she gets back, he decided, I'll get her out of here.

He looked dazedly about at the other customers, all seamy

and scarred and hard-bitten. A dive like this could be raided anytime. And if Henshaw happened to be picked up in a raid and Uncle Waldo got wind of it, that puritanical old gentleman could be counted on not only to fire Henshaw but to disinherit him as well.

He brought his right hand up to his forehead. The hand that Hattie had held a moment before, he remembered. They'd had a second together. A second that was wholly theirs. And Hattie was warm and kind and human. Not like Maria who alternately set him on fire and then quenched the flame of his ardor, leaving him vaporous.

Deep shadow fell across the table. Henshaw looked up. A waiter with a scarred chin pressed a bit of paper into Henshaw's palm, turned and moved away. Henshaw straightened out the paper, stared dully at the words written in scarlet lipstick.

DON'T WAIT. H.

A sharp pang of disappointment pricked through the numbness as Henshaw let the note flutter to the table. His eyes scouted the dingy room. He didn't see Hattie. He didn't even see anybody who resembled Hattie, and it occurred to him that he might possibly never see another woman like Hattie if he lived to be a hundred.

"But that's life," he sighed aloud and stood unsteadily. He pushed a cigarette into his lips and then didn't seem to be able to find his lighter. He took the paper folder of matches out of the ash tray and moved toward the exit.

Henshaw climbed six narrow concrete steps to an aisle

between buildings at street level and groped his way toward the dim night glow along Canal Street. Halfway along the passage, he came to a swaying stop. Eyes now used to the gloom, he could see somebody crouching at the mouth of the passage.

Henshaw fell back against the building wall, flattened himself against the bricks as the crouching figure straightened. A man. Somebody slight and short, his back toward Henshaw. Something metallic flashed in the man's hand. A white handkerchief flaunted—a wiping motion? The man turned and peered into the black slot where Henshaw was hidden.

The face of the man was a pale, narrow wedge. V for Violence. And then it was gone.

As footsteps receded into silence, Henshaw peeled himself away from the wall, moved out to the street, stopped, clutched blindly, and reeled against the building corner. There was somebody down there. At his feet. A body. Henshaw sank down onto his knees, brought out the paper matches, and struck one.

The girl lay on her back, a dark wetness of blood on the front of her dress. With her bright rouged lips apart. With her eyes half open and glazed in the flickering matchlight. Someone he knew. Hattie.

"Hattie!" He felt the shape of her name along his lips. He stood on caving knees. Somewhere, deep in the heart of the city, a clock chimed the hour of 3:00 A.M. A death knell for Hattie. Minutes ago she'd been alive and warm. The touch of her hand had been warm and lasting. And now....

A sob rose in Henshaw's throat. Why in the name of heaven

hadn't he got her out of that dive when the impulse first struck him?

The match dropped from his shaking fingers. The darkness crowded in upon him and with it came panic. He had to get out of here. Right now. He couldn't have his name associated with anything like this. Couldn't have Uncle Waldo's eagle eye light on a newspaper account of a murder that involved Arthur Henshaw.

He sidled, stumbled about, and broke into a run.

IT WASN'T until an hour later that Henshaw began to worry about his cigarette lighter. Suppose that when Hattie had swept the snapshots into her bag she'd absently got hold of the lighter as well? It wasn't monogrammed, but it did have the crest of his college fraternity on the face of it. Suppose it was found and could be identified as his?

But then, it couldn't, he assured himself. There were hundreds of lighters like that. He was all right. *He* was. But stronger than fear was the sense of guilt that dogged him. How in the hell could he have run out on Hattie and left her there alone, lying dead on the pavement?

But it's done now, he told himself, and I've got to forget it. I've *got* to, and I'm going to.

It kept coming back. Little bits of it floated back like refuse from a shipwreck. First, there was Sam Dawson's face. Henshaw saw it, two days later, looking out at him from the front page of an Indianapolis newspaper. The same narrow, pale face.

Sam Dawson, ex-con who had recently completed a prison term for forgery, had been arrested for the murder of Hattie

McClaren, his former sweetheart, on the night of March 27th. The same old story. Hattie hadn't waited for Sam. He'd discovered her with somebody else. And he'd used a knife.

Henshaw quickly turned the page. Forget about it. They had the right man, he'd get the chair, and the thing to do was to forget about it.

It wasn't until the day the Grand Jury considered the McClaren case that Henshaw had the rotten luck to run into Roscoe Brun in a Pennsylvania Street bar.

Major Brun—he had served with Army Intelligence at one time or another and insisted on retaining his former title—was a short, thick-bodied man with a wiry brush of close-cropped gray hair, a full, ruddy face, and an overbearing personality. He had collected in book form the stories of a dozen famous murder trials into which he had managed to inject himself as an authority on the subject.

"I should hate to be in Dawson's shoes," Brun began, salting his beer. "That girl really hung one on him. Whole thing is reminiscent of the Ferratti case. You've read my book *Man About Murder*, haven't you?"

"Look," Henshaw said with a show of impatience, "never mind about the Ferratti case. This other thing. Who hung what on whom?"

"The McClaren girl. She named Dawson before she died."

The back-bar mirror caught Henshaw's face—round, boyish for a man of thirty-five, and right now sickly pale. He said, "I thought she was dead—that is, didn't I read she was dead when they found her?"

"Oh, no," the self-recognized authority contradicted. "They kept her alive long enough to name Dawson." Major Brun watched with seeming interest while Henshaw's shaking hands scratched a match for a cigarette. "What happened to your lighter, Arthur?"

"It—it's out of fluid," Henshaw stammered. He slid off the stool and moved blindly toward the door. Good lord, he thought, she was alive when I found her! With all that blood? With that varnished look her eyes had? I might have helped her. She might have lived. But how the hell was I to know? I'm a drygoods salesman, not a doctor. She probably would have died even if I had gone for help. I've got to forget it. I can't let it bother me.

But then it did bother him. It was a recurring nightmare—her eyes looking up at him, less glazed than reproachful. Suppose the reason she had walked out on him was that she hadn't wanted to involve him with jealous Sam Dawson. She was warm and human and kind, and she might have figured on getting Dawson away from the place before he could make trouble that would involve Henshaw. And for that, she'd died.

THEN THERE was that damned annoying business about the lighter. Had the police found the lighter? Was that what Major Brun had been driving at?

Personal fear and a sense of guilt—they both bothered him. Like that night of April 11th when Henshaw took Maria Renard to the theatre and then for a late supper at Club #7— Maria of the beautiful long green eyes that could get into him and reduce him to quivering pulp.

Henshaw looked across the table at Maria and found himself suddenly thinking of the dead girl, Hattie McClaren.

"What's wrong, Arthur?"

Maria's velvet voice startled Henshaw. The hand he put out toward one of the three drinks he'd ordered before the liquor curfew trembled coarsely. He felt a little sick. He pushed back from the table, mumbled an apology as he turned and found his way past the stage where the band was playing its closing set of numbers.

He entered the men's room, bent over one of the three lavatories, and doused his face with cold water. Behind him there was a skittering sound along the floor followed by a solid *thuck*. Henshaw, his face dripping, looked around, but he couldn't locate the source of the sound and the room was apparently empty.

Close to him a voice called him by name. The room was empty.

Henshaw stepped away from the drier and put a cigarette into his mouth. His eyes traveled down to the door of the men's room, came to rest on a thin pine wedge driven in between the floor and the door bottom. *He* hadn't wedged the door shut, and there was no one else who could have.

"Henshaw, I want to talk to you."

The voice again, patient but relentless. The voice from nowhere.

Well, nuts! Henshaw thought. When I get out into the crowd, I'll be all right.

"Would you like a light for that cigarette?"

11

The voice, directly behind him. Henshaw turned slowly, his back to the door, and his eyeballs crawled from their lids. Five feet from the floor and with no visible means of support, a cigarette lighter floated towards him. Not just any cigarette lighter, but one with a Phi Delt emblem on its face. If it wasn't his, it was one just like his.

The cigarette fell from his lips. He snatched at the cigarette lighter only to see the thing dance away in the air and finally fall to the floor. He started toward it. Something caught hold of his upper arms and held him rigidly. He stared down at the sleeves of his Tuxedo. The dark cloth was crumpled in the clutch of—fingers?

Quiet mocking laughter. Then, *"Now do you believe in Captain Zero?"*

ZERO. PENDLEVILLE. The name and the city were immediately associated in Henshaw's mind. Something he'd read in the papers months ago about Pendleville—a gang war, wasn't it, and something about rotten city politics? Whatever it was, the crime wave had paled into insignificance beside the fantastic story of a man calling himself Captain Zero who had somehow mastered the secret of invisibility and who had single-handedly brought Pendleville's collection of criminals to justice.

Fingers he couldn't see were hooked deeply into his biceps. Close to his starting eyes were two pin-points of light, reflections, possibly, and beyond that the blurred wall of the lavatory—nothing else. Yet Henshaw was clearly, painfully conscious of a being of strength and substance. He could feel warm breath against his sweating face.

"You're going to talk to me, Henshaw," the quiet voice spoke. *"What is it you've got on your mind you're afraid I'll reach?"*

Henshaw didn't, couldn't answer. He was released suddenly, caught by the shoulder, spun, tripped to the tile floor. Landing on the back of his lap, Henshaw started to get up, his eyes darting about.

"Right here," the voice said. *"Above you. Don't try to get up. You're not going anywhere. Why did you snatch at that lighter? Is it yours?"*

Henshaw shook his head vigorously. "I—I—that is, I don't know. I lost one like it." He tried to get up again, but something—a foot, perhaps—pushed against his chest. "Why pick on me?" Henshaw's voice approached a whine. "I'm not a crook. I'm just a drygoods salesman."

"You're a yellow rat," the voice said deliberately. *"You arrived in Pendleville the evening of March 27th, didn't you?"*

"Yah—yes."

"You checked in at the Park Hotel at 8:15 P.M., got a sample room, opened your cases to be ready to do business the following morning. Yet you checked out of the hotel eight hours later."

"I—I—" Henshaw moistened his lips. "I had to get back to Indianapolis. I got a telegram."

"No, you didn't. I checked on that. You were hitting the dives along Canal Street that night, and you saw Sam Dawson knife the McClaren girl, didn't you?"

"No, no," Henshaw protested. "I'd have called the police if I'd seen anything like that. The police have Dawson, haven't they?"

13

"They've got Dawson," the voice of Zero replied. *"And you'd better pray that Dawson gets the chair,"* the quiet voice said. *"Otherwise he just might be seeing you. He just might, at that. In any event, I will. And don't say you'll be seeing me. You won't."*

Henshaw shivered.

CHAPTER 2
THE MAN IN THE BLACK HAT

I N A room on the top floor of a building just north of Indianapolis' Monument Circle a man sat at a drop-head desk. He wore a black pork-pie hat with a wide brim pulled low to shadow the upper portion of his face. His chin was hidden in the turned-up collar of a dark topcoat.

Except for the desk and its chair the room was barren and dimly lighted. The floor was of oiled pine that, in that area surrounding the desk, seemed to have been patched with some sort of sheet metal, worn and dull.

The Man in the Black Hat raised a black gloved hand to a panel mounted on the drop-head portion of the desk, touched a switch and then a dial. A red pilot light glowed above a meter. The man spoke into a microphone, his voice nasal, metallic, without inflection.

"GHQ calling Number Three. Calling Number Three. Calling Number Three. GHQ calling. Come in Number Three."

Again the gloved fingers touched a switch. From the grill of a small loud-speaker set in the panel came a crackling sound that built into the recognizable throb of a car engine. A man was talking.

"Honestly, Maria, I'm mad about you."

Maria Renard laughed softly. "You don't quite know me, Arthur," her velvet voice spoke from the loudspeaker. "Not actually."

The Man in the Black Hat jerked up a pencil. "Quite," he said, rapidly writing on a sheet of paper. "Actually." *Quite, actually*—key words in the code. He chuckled. A clever woman, Number Three. Once upon a time she had been the all-important part of a vaudeville mind reading act. Thus it was possible for her to code a message to him and at the same time converse with the man called Arthur with whom she was driving. Arthur, whoever he was, would not be on sufficiently intimate terms with Maria to know that she had, concealed upon her lovely person, a flat plastic case like that of a hearing aid and which contained the minute radio receiving and transmitting instrument.

And Maria would be extremely careful that Arthur never got close enough to the gold button that apparently ornamented her right ear but which was actually a sensitive bone conduction receiver.

The Man in the Black Hat listened to the conversation until he heard Maria's key word, "Really?" which stood for "Standing by." Then he glanced down the list of code words which he had written and rapidly translated:

WILL REPORT LATER.

"Like hell you will!" he said aloud into the lonely room. His gloved hands flashed across the panel. His voice, still metallic, was taut as a guitar string as he spoke to the girl in the car:

"Report immediately, Number Three. In person. At GHQ." And then he added after a short pause, "Or else."

A clever woman, he thought, but obstinate. She needed discipline. Had she not been so damned beautiful he would have given her a lesson long ago.

He again switched over to Receiving in time to hear Maria say, "Don't be funny." And it was impossible for him to know whether this had been intended for his ears or for Arthur's....

IT OCCURRED to Maria Renard now, as it often had before, that The Man in the Black Hat might be a very attractive person. For that reason she put on a slight yet wholly provocative smile as the brilliant light from a ceiling fixture flooded down upon her. She was sitting in an unfurnished office adjoining the GHQ of the Man in the Black Hat, facing a mirror made of one-way "Argus" glass. From the other side, the Man in the Black Hat watched her, studying her intently. Then he spoke.

"Number Three," the metallic voice said—entirely void of emotion. "I have been trying to contact you since mid-afternoon."

"I'm sorry," she said contritely, eyelids fluttering. "But I had a headache." She touched a heavy gold earclip with gloved fingers. "These things can be a beastly annoyance when you've a headache."

There was a long and possibly disapproving silence during which Maria returned the steady gaze of her own reflection and

"GHQ calling Number Three. Come in, Number Three," The Man in the Black Hat said.

imagined that she was under the closest scrutiny of the Man in the Black Hat.

"You're not angry?"

"No-o—"

It was the first time that the voice had ever indicated hesitation or uncertainty. Perhaps, Maria thought, Mr. Black Hat had begun to notice that Number Three was an attractive woman—not merely a wheel within a wheel within a wheel.

"Number Three, you will leave immediately for Pendleville. There Number Fifteen will contact you. The assignment ought not to be too difficult, all things considered."

Her eyes widened somewhat. "And the assignment?"

"In brief, a man by the name of Samuel Dawson is to be tried on the charge of murder in the criminal court at Pendleville. Dawson's talents are required by our organization. The verdict returned must be that of not guilty. Number Fifteen has assured us of the selection of one James Oliver as foreman of the jury. Oliver is a man of considerable influence, capable of swaying the others whichever way he wishes."

"Then James Oliver is one of us?" the woman asked.

The Man in the Black Hat uttered a dry laugh. "Hardly. James Oliver is your objective. He must be reached. It so happens that he is extremely susceptible to charming women."

That again, Maria Renard thought distastefully. The toe of her satin slipper tapped in annoyance on the hard base floor.

"I do not expect you to resort to bribery except as a last resort," the voice of the man behind the mirror went on, "but if you do, funds will be made available. You are to make absolutely certain that James Oliver is our man. If you fail you will be—removed."

Beneath her fur piece Maria Renard's shoulders shuddered slightly.

"You will be given protection by our organization at all times," the Man in the Black Hat promised, "but I wish to leave with you one final word of caution."

"Yes?"

"To be quite literal, that one word is *Zero*."

Maria Renard took a shallow breath. "I—understand."

"Then that is all."

CHAPTER 3
MURDER BOULEVARD

DORO KELLY of the Pendleville *World* tossed two inches of smoldering cigarette to the floor of the criminal courtroom and on her next long-legged stride put the toe of her brown pump upon the glowing tip and ground it out. She did all this with drop-kick precision that did not alter her measured pacing back and forth in front of the row of seats that had been reserved for the press.

She was rather tall, lithe, with black hair done in a short, pert bob, with eyes that varied disconcertingly from blue to green, with a short and—in her opinion—ridiculous nose, tip-tilted and bridged with freckles. Her straight skirted suit was spice brown and, she had discovered to her dismay, inclined to wrinkle.

But then, she thought, I'm wrinkling too. Two more hours of this and I'll be a hag.

It was now nearly four o'clock on the afternoon of April 20. Two hours ago Judge Nathan Masters had concluded his charge, and the seven men and five women composing the jury had straggled up from their chairs as though not too willing to face the responsibility which lay ahead of them.

James Oliver, the foreman, a dapper, middle-aged man, had paused at the door leading to the jury room. His thin-lipped mouth had twitched slightly—the beginning of a smile, a grimace, or perhaps it was only an indication of nervousness.

And at the threshold of another door, the prisoner, Samuel

Dawson, had glanced up at the hovering defense attorney Reg Nolan. A confident smirk had crossed Dawson's narrow, mottled face, and then he had stepped briskly through the opening.

Why the smirk? Doro Kelly wondered. They've got you, Mr. Dawson, right where the hair is short. In spite of all the razzle-dazzle your big-town attorney tried to pull, they've got you.

Reg Nolan, from Indianapolis, had not been impressive until his final plea when he had taken his thin shadow of a doubt and spread it out to resemble a total eclipse. Through cross examination of the prosecution's witnesses, Nolan had managed to emphasize a single technical omission: that no doctor had actually told the late Hattie McClaren that she was going to die.

"As though anyone could actually be that inhuman!" Doro had whispered to Lee Allyn, also from the *World*.

According to Nolan there was grave doubt that Hattie's naming Sam Dawson ought to be construed as a death-bed accusation. Why, Nolan managed to imply, she might have been calling upon good old Sam, her own true love, to save her.

Nolan, a tawny-haired giant with a sullen face and a voice worthy of a Shakespearian tragedian, had done a good job with what he had, but evidence was so overwhelmingly against Sam Dawson that Doro Kelly could not conceive of any jury returning a verdict other than guilty.

During the first hour after the jury had retired the crowded courtroom had been alive with rumor and speculation. Now weariness had set in. At least one person in Doro Kelly's immediate vicinity had gone to sleep.

SHE PAUSED in her pacing to consider Mr. Lee Allyn, who lounged incredibly on the hard oak seat immediately to the right of the one assigned to her. His head was tipped forward, his eyes closed, his horn-rimmed glasses pushed up onto his undistinguished forehead to the roots of his very blond hair. He was small and thin and neat. In a crowd of five you were inclined not to notice him at all. When he was asleep, as he very frequently was in the *World* office, Doro thought she saw a certain strength, a fullness of purpose about the young man's lean jaw.

"Sleepy Lee Allyn," Doro said, and when he did not waken she looked at him, her Irish mouth compressed, and wondered what would happen if she kicked him on his skinny shins. Lee Allyn was rather a nice boy. Ineffectual sometimes, but sweet. She often thought, somewhat resignedly, that she'd end up marrying him. Or she would go to the opposite extreme and marry Ed Cavanaugh, Pendleville's young and vigorous police chief.

But until she decided between the two she could dream, couldn't she, of strong, unseen arms that once had held her? She could dream of that quiet, oddly compelling voice of Captain Zero that once had called her "Angel."

Doro Kelly leaned over to grasp Lee Allyn's shoulder and shake him.

"Wake up, boy."

"Uh—hm?" Allyn started awake, and that suggestion of strength that Doro had noticed in his face flowed away leaving a stupidity stranded about the gaping mouth and the weak, pale blue eyes. Eyes which, previous to a delicate operation eight years before, had been stone blind.

Allyn sat up straight, brought his glasses down where they belonged. He glanced at Judge Masters' empty bench, the equally empty jury box, and then at his watch. He was always looking at his watch, not because it was mere habit but because time meant more to him than it meant to the average man.

"Lee, I want to ask you something," Doro Kelly said.

He smiled at her, a kind of hungering smile. "Lady, I am overwhelmed."

"When the jury went out, why did you say, 'Watch Oliver?'"

Allyn blinked owlishly as though not at all sure. "Well, he seemed nervous to me, that's all." His eyes slipped away from her and noticed a short, heavy-set man coming in their direction across the front of the courtroom. Allyn leaned forward, reached in front of Doro Kelly, and touched a reporter named Mack Trimble on the arm.

"Isn't that your pal, Roscoe Brun?"

Mack snorted. "The Major? Friend? Oh, sure!" He watched the heavy-set man with ill-disguised contempt in his eyes. "Look at that suit, will you!"

Brun's suit was gabardine and it so closely approached a military tan that it came within brass buttons of being a uniform. His full, ruddy face had a shine to it as though well preserved against the ravages of time by a thin coating of wax.

Doro Kelly asked, "What makes him like that, Mack?"

Trimble said, "Lord knows. Maybe it's because he wrote a book once, the ten thousand sold copies of which amount to a tremendous strain on the floor joists of his attic. That strut he must have learned from those homing pigeons he raises. He'll travel a thousand miles to sit in on a murder trial, and if I didn't get paid for it I wouldn't go across the street."

Trimble turned to the Major. "We'd like to have your opinion on the pending verdict, Major."

"Can't give it," was Brun's crisp and surprising reply. "There will be no verdict reached here today. A hung jury. From my experience I should say that's rather obvious."

Brun moved off. At that moment the door to the left of the witness box opened and the tall, stern figure of Judge Nathan Masters appeared. Cigarettes disappeared. The room sighed collectively.

Through the right hand door Sam Dawson appeared, less cocky perhaps, his face more mottled, and with him the sullen, lion-maned man who was Reg Nolan.

FROM THE door behind the seat of justice the seven men and five women who composed the jury were filing to stand before their respective chairs. Some looked exhausted, others resigned, and one, a coarse-featured, red-faced man, coughed self-consciously.

The foreman, James Oliver, took out a tan breast pocket handkerchief and daubed at a pallid brow. He wavered slightly on his feet and clutched the oak rail in front of him.

"Ladies and gentlemen of the jury, have you reached a verdict?"

Twelve voice in chorus husked, "We have."

"Foreman, how do you find as to the defendant Samuel Dawson—guilty, or not guilty?"

"Your honor—" James Oliver's voice caught. For an instant his gaze wavered from Sam Dawson's mottled face, lifted, flicked across the gallery at the back of the court room. Following Oliver's eyes, Lee Allyn saw something in the gallery—a flutter of white as though a handkerchief were waved. And then his attention was drawn back to the jury box as James Oliver's voice struggled up out of silence.

"Not guilty."

The crowd took a breath and with it uttered a sound that was like a groan of protest. There was movement, first a gentle wave restrained by the pounding of Judge Masters' gavel and then a sudden surge toward the doors. Somewhere, surely, there must be fresher, cleaner air than this!

Lee Allyn was caught in the tide of news reporters rushing to the 'phones. He glimpsed Doro Kelly's pretty face pale with shock, her lips compressed against an angry outburst.

"You take it, angel," Allyn called to her. "I got things to do." And then he turned and fought through to the center aisle. Actually, he didn't give a damn what went through to the *World* city desk. He was thinking of that flash of white handkerchief up in the gallery the instant James Oliver had faltered. A signal? A warning? It could be anything—or nothing at all.

He had gained the narrow stairway beneath the gallery now and waited at the foot of it, an inconspicuous figure plastered against the wall, frequently jostled but seldom noticed even by people who knew him well. Behind his horn-rimmed glasses his pale eyes darted from face to face without knowing for whom he searched nor what he expected to find.

Lee Allyn's thin cheeks warmed in an angry flush as he recognized Arthur Henshaw. Henshaw had known something about the McClaren girl's murder, something that he had willfully concealed. That was now obvious. His conscience-stricken eyes involuntarily touched a gray-haired woman who had reached the foot of the stairs.

"Oh, Hattie, Hattie," the mother sobbed. "My little girl! Nobody cares. Not nobody!" She tottered forward as the big cop who was posted at the door moved sympathetically over to help her.

At the same time, Arthur Henshaw's lagging steps came to a complete stop. He grasped at, but blindly missed, the handrail as his knees started caving. He went down in slow motion, slid a little way, and then lodged crosswise of the stairs.

"Hey, officer!" a man called excitedly. "Fella's fainted. Must be the heat in this building."

Lee Allyn thought grimly that Arthur Henshaw didn't know what heat was. Not yet he didn't.

THE MURDERER, acquitted but a murderer still, had posed before the news photographers, then he went on out, stood for a moment buttoning his natty gray topcoat.

On the courthouse steps, his back to the limestone railing, a newshawk stood, a paunchy figure in a dirty gray sweater and greasy gray cap. A blind man's white cane hung over his left arm. He cocked his head as Sam Dawson's footsteps approached.

"Paper, Mister? All about the murder trial."

Sam Dawson laughed harshly. "N' thanks."

"Better have one, Mister," the newshawk said in a low voice. "It's on the house. Compliments of The Hat." He shoved a folded paper into Sam Dawson's hand in such a way that Sam could not fail to grasp it in the approximate middle.

As Dawson's fingers closed he realized that this was more than a paper. Much more. Something was concealed within— something of a size and shape familiar to Sam Dawson.

"Read… all… about… it," the newshawk shouted, but for Dawson's ears alone. "All about the murder trial."

For an instant, Dawson caught a glimpse of the supposedly blind eyes beneath the bill of the greasy cap. One of them winked. A dirty palm was thrust out to Dawson, and while Dawson went through the motions of dropping a coin into it, he received a bit of whispered advice.

"Muddy panel truck. It's the getaway. Watch for it."

"Keep the change," Dawson said aloud and tucked the folded paper under his arm.

"Read… all… about… it!" The newsboy shouted as Dawson moved on down the stone steps. Dawson thought, Sure, I get you. He brought the paper out, let the small black automatic slide into his right palm. Then he unfurled the paper to its front page.

"Geez!" Dawson said under his breath. *"Now,* they mean? Right here?" His squint eyes glanced nervously across the street at the building that housed the Pendleville police headquarters. AT 4:35 Lee Allyn hurried out of the same side door of the courthouse. Ahead of him, now on the sidewalk and walking north at a brisk pace, was James Oliver, foreman of the jury that had acquitted Dawson. As Lee Allyn went down the steps he glimpsed the paunchy newshawk in the gray sweater.

"Hi, Ben," Allyn flung over his shoulder.

"Hi," Ben said, and Allyn paused, right foot on the bottom step, to glance back at the man in the gray sweater. Queer that Ben hadn't said, "Hi, Mr. Allyn." He usually did. None understood better than Lee Allyn the pride the blind take in recognizing persons by their voices and footsteps. Just as blind Lee Allyn had known the customers who came regularly to his father's fruit store in Chicago, so blind Ben Keeler knew all the people who frequented the courthouse in Pendleville.

For a second Allyn lingered at the foot of the courthouse steps, bothered by the uneasy notion that the man in the gray sweater was not Ben Keeler. Then he glanced up the street and saw James Oliver rapidly pulling away from him.

And at the same instant Allyn saw another figure approaching from the opposite direction—a man in a natty gray topcoat who was apparently engrossed in a newspaper which he held up in front of his face. A pair of narrow eyes peered over the top of the paper and then were quickly averted. Sam Dawson's.

Lee Allyn drew a short, quick breath and broke into a sprint. Had he looked back then, he would have seen the mud-stained black panel delivery truck that jockeyed for position in the stream of traffic. He would have seen the supposed blind news peddler grip his white cane and hurry in the same direction Allyn had taken.

But for the moment Allyn's chief concern was for James

Oliver, who was walking on oblivious to the fact that the eyes that watched him over the newspaper were those of Sam Dawson.

When Oliver was ten feet in front of Dawson the little gun showed its ugly snout from beneath the folded edge of the newspaper, aimed low for a belly shot. Oliver didn't see it. If he had, he might have doubted his senses, for this was the man whose life he had saved that same afternoon.

And then the little gun was yapping like a vicious terrier—three stuttering shots, a fourth placed more deliberately as Oliver's legs crumpled. The April afternoon was hideous with noise—gunfire, screams, glass crashing, and metal tearing as a car skewed sideways and caused a pile-up.

Dawson placed his fifth shot, the clincher, into the sprawled figure on the sidewalk. He backed off, crouched over, his kill-crazy eyes alert. He saw Lee Allyn bearing down on him.

He swiveled the gun and jerked the trigger. Allyn heard the high thin whine of the bullet. Then, hurdling Oliver's body, he launched himself in a long tackle that struck Dawson thigh-high and cut him down.

Dawson's knees caught Allyn in the chest and knocked the wind out of him. Gasping, Allyn's left hand went up, clutched at an empty newspaper. Then something fell on Allyn's head. Something like the courthouse.

He had no way of knowing it was the loaded handle of a white cane that had knocked him out.

CHAPTER 4
BARRICADE

T HE TRAFFIC pile-up had not been intentional. The gaunt-faced man at the wheel of the mud-stained panel truck, momentarily disconcerted, jammed on his brakes and brought the truck to a lurching stop five feet behind the car in front of him.

"Now what the hell do I do?" he said aloud and half expected to hear the metallic voice of the Man in the Black Hat coming to him from the little black button behind his left ear lobe.

But there was no help from The Hat. He saw the sidewalk, deserted except for three men struggling. He cursed, slammed at the gear shift lever, cramped the front wheels sharply to the right to buck the curb. As he pulled the truck up onto the sidewalk, one of the men concealed in the paneled body behind him unlimbered the submachine gun and shot through the slots in the armor plate lining the rear doors of the truck. That meant trouble with the cops.

On the sidewalk, the fake blind man saw the truck bearing down on him. He caned Lee Allyn and helped Sam Dawson extricate himself from Allyn's arms. The truck was in the clear now. It bounced down off the curb, slowed, but did not stop rolling. Dawson and the other came aboard, falling over each other into paneled body.

"Damned tight!" somebody said. And then the submachine gun laid down another barrage. Two motorcycle police had got through the tangle. They were throwing .38 calibre slugs at the only vulnerable part of the truck—its tires. Immediately ahead, the street intersection loomed, cleared by police sirens.

The driver of the panel truck swung to the left, into the middle of the street, and jammed the gas pedal to the floor. In the rear vision mirror he caught a glimpse of a police motorcycle as it careened madly across the street to crash riderless into a parked car.

The truck driver smiled grimly.

"Number Ten."

The voice, that of a woman, came from the black button behind the truck driver's left earlobe.

"This is Number Three calling Ten. Report position."

Position not so hot, the truck driver thought as his right hand left the wheel long enough to touch a switch on the side of the plastic case on his coat front.

"Going west on Morris," he reported. "Third block from Main. No visible pursuers. Not now. Come in Number Three."

"Instructions: Go through barricade on Fourth. This street is clear. Go north to Elm, then west to creek. Bridge is mined. Proceed as planned. That is all."

Fourth was the next street. Number Ten saw the barricade—three of the street commissioner's white-painted half-trestles. He swung the truck to the right, his left rear wheel knocking over one of the trestles. Ahead, the street was all clear.

TWENTY SECONDS after the panel truck had gone through the barricade, the long black sedan that carried the police chief's shield on its radiator grill came to the intersection of Morris and Fourth. Bristow, the driver, applied the brakes, glancing at the dark, wooden-Indian profile of the man beside him.

Chief-of-Police Ed Cavanaugh cupped the microphone of the two-way FM police radio in his left hand, and with his right motioned ahead to indicate the upset barricade.

"That street isn't closed," he snapped. "Go on through, and give it hell."

Cavanaugh had picked up the original alarm while heading toward his own apartment. This was one of those rare things called a break. He thumbed the switch button on the mike handle and addressed the radio dispatcher at headquarters.

"This is Cavanaugh. On code twelve, panel truck believed traveling north on Fourth. Block all highways and county roads leading from city. Dispatch all available squads to north sector."

Cavanaugh glanced down at the speedometer. The needle was climbing rapidly now that Bristow had a clear street in front of him. Cavanaugh thought grimly that the trick with the street department's barricades was working as much to the advantage of the police as it had to the criminals.

Gordon Street. Cottage Avenue, Rockwood, Haviland— Cavanaugh glimpsed the street signs as the black car ripped off block after block. Elm Street—

Cavanaugh yelled, "Whoa!" and threw up a forearm to brace himself against the instrument panel as Bristow tramped down on the brakes. Tortured rubber screamed.

"Dust," Cavanaugh said. "Didn't you see it? Elm Street isn't paved. It's got to be them. That barricade gag wasn't too smart."

Bristow made a loop turn in mid-block by jouncing over the

sidewalk curb. "Sorry I missed it, Chief," he said. "I was watching for kids. You can't tell about kids."

Cavanaugh said, "You keep watching for kids. Right at Elm." He hung the mike on its fork on the radio panel and pulled his police positive. Just as surely as they had seen the dust hanging in the air from the panel truck, so the criminals would see the dust that now was kicking up from the wheels of the police car.

Elm Street was part of a new real estate development, the houses thinly spaced. It reached from Fourth Street down to the creek, a distance of about eight blocks. Against the green line of trees that grew along the creek bank, Cavanaugh saw the moving cloud of brown dust. The truck.

He said dryly to Bristow, "Pick up your feet."

The driver gave more gas and the speedometer started to climb above fifty. Now fifty-five, sixty, sixty-five. The street was narrow, treacherous with a deep, loose surface of gravel.

"There's a hell of a bridge off here," Bristow said.

Cavanaugh knew the bridge. He saw it up ahead, a rusty steel span that arched above concrete abutments. He saw at the same time the mud-stained panel truck as it rolled down from the center of the bridge. He glanced at the speedometer now quivering at seventy.

"Pick 'em up, Bristow. There's a Y on the other side of that bridge. They'll have to go either south or north. They'll make a nice target from the bridge if you can get us within range."

Bristow opened the throttle wide, and at that instant both he and Cavanaugh saw the huge orange-red flame shoot upward against the dark line of trees along the creek two hundred yards ahead. Against the flare the rusty span of the bridge heaved and buckled. They heard and felt the earth-quaking roar of the explosion as the twisted girders settled down into the creek.

Bristow rammed at the brake pedal, released it as the car skewed on loose gravel. He gave a spurt of gas, felt the rear wheels dig in and hold onto the narrow road. But at this speed the concrete abutment of the bridge seemed to be hurtling toward them. He braked again, full weight on the pedal.

There was a final, sickening lurch, a crash, a jarring end to all motion as the front end crumpled against concrete. The bonnet ripped off and folded back like a paper boxlid. Bristow kept riding the brake pedal. Then he sank back onto the cushions and looked at Cavanaugh.

Cavanaugh was having trouble with a sprung door. He cursed impotently, kicked and beat against it, finally got it open. He jumped out, limping, ran forward to the bridge approach which rose eight feet above the level of the road. He stood there, staring at nothing. The panel truck was gone.

Bristow joined him. He said, his voice a bit shaky, "That's very un-good, huh Chief?"

Cavanaugh did not reply. The thing was stunning in its magnitude, in the perfection of its planning, in the clockwork precision of its execution.

"And," he said, "the damned ruthlessness of it—whatever it is."

IF CAVANAUGH was impressed by the workings of the getaway scheme, killer Sam Dawson was doubly so. Scooped up as he had been from what had developed into the hottest spot of his criminal career, Dawson found himself in the semi-dark interior of the panel truck. There was machine gun clatter, and Dawson had supposed he would be given a gun and told to help with the running fight. Instead, a calm voice which he recognized as that of the phony blind man had given him an order.

"Strip to your shorts, Dawson."

"Yeah?" Dawson yammered. He was thrown against the side of the truck as it swung around the corner. Now he could just make out the figure of the machine gunner at the rear of the truck through daylight that seeped through slots in armor plate.

"Cripes!" Dawson said. "An armored car! Some class. Just like Al Capone had once."

The blind man laughed. "Capone was a piker, Dawson. Have you got those clothes off yet?"

Dawson had to admit that he hadn't yet begun to undress. He wanted to know why he should.

"Because I said so," the other man replied. "And I say so because Number Ten just told me. And Number Ten told me because he got it from GHQ."

Dawson started to peel. "Yeah? Who's GHQ—the Black Hat, huh?"

"Not necessarily," said the other cryptically and began to help Dawson remove his clothing.

Dawson chuckled. "I get it. *You're* Mr. Hat."

"Don't be funny. I'm Number Fifteen. I'm just a wheel within a wheel. I don't even think Black Hat is in on this caper at all. Now hold still and stop asking questions. I've got to spray you with some stuff that'll change your complexion."

Dawson leaned against the inner wall of the truck. There was no shooting now, and the going was smooth and swift. In the dim light he could see Number Fifteen, also naked to the waist, bending over a paint spray outfit. Dawson heard the throb of a compressor, and then Number Fifteen straightened with the spray gun in his hand.

"This'll feel cold," Number Fifteen warned, "but they say a slab in the morgue is colder."

The fine mist slapped Dawson's chest like so much sleet. When he'd stopped gasping, Number Fifteen raised the muzzle of the spray gun and thoroughly covered Dawson's face and hair.

"Turn around," he ordered. Dawson turned and took the sprayed liquid on his shoulders, neck, and arms.

"Okay," Number Fifteen said. "That'll dry in about fifteen seconds. Try not to get yourself smeared. And if you can't think of anything better to do while I'm spraying myself, you can brush up on your Southern accent."

As soon as Number Fifteen had turned off the spray machine he shoved a bundle of clothing into Dawson's hands.

The man at the wheel of the truck opened a slide at the rear of the cab and called to Number Fifteen. The latter moved forward, stood for a moment while the truck driver addressed him in low tones. Then Fifteen moved back where Dawson was struggling to get his feet into a pair of stiff, thick-soled work-shoes.

"We picked up a tail somewhere," Fifteen announced. He went back to the gunner, said something, then returned to the center of the truck where he too put on overalls.

Dawson felt the truck climb a short, steep incline. Then it

rumbled across a bridge, swung sharply to the left, and came to an abrupt stop.

"What's wrong?" Dawson asked excitedly.

Number Fifteen laughed. "Not a damned thing. Nothing ever goes wrong on these deals, fella."

Dawson looked anxiously toward the rear of the truck as the gunner opened the door and sprang out onto the road. Dawson could hear the man moving around in the weeds along the shoulder and then he reappeared, a tall, blond young man with a stolid countenance.

"Let's go," the gunner sang out to the driver, and the truck started to roll.

THEN THERE was the roar of the explosion. Dawson let out a startled oath and made an instinctive snatch for the gun he didn't have. Number Fifteen dropped a hand on Dawson's shoulder.

"The bridge was mined," he explained. "Now everything is okay. We're heading back to Pendleville."

"Pendleville?" Dawson gasped.

"Sure. You don't really think the cops would let us get outside the city limits, do you? They'll have every road and highway blocked by this time. They've got radios too, don't forget."

"Then what'll we do?" Dawson asked, his voice not quite steady.

"Do?" Number Fifteen repeated. "What we always do. Whatever GHQ tells us to do. When you've been in this outfit for a while you'll realize that it doesn't pay to worry too much about your immediate future. You're either taken care of by GHQ or you don't have any immediate future."

"This GHQ—I don't get it."

"General Headquarters," Number Fifteen replied impatiently. "It makes with the orders via radio. You do what you're told, and you don't get into trouble. Black Hat's got a mobile unit in this sector. He gives his orders to the sector officer and she relays them to us."

"She? You mean a dame is running this caper?"

"For Black Hat—yes. Now just relax, can't you?"

Dawson couldn't relax. There was a slow trembling within him that he couldn't master. Because this thing was so big—so much bigger than he had ever imagined. There had been rumors, these past two years in stir, of a new and vast criminal organization that had extended into every state in the nation, but Dawson hadn't supposed it was anything like this.

And now he was in it. He was a wheel in the thing. He might even get to be a—what was it Number Fifteen had called the dame? A sector officer? He might even get to be—

His speculation was interrupted by the sudden stop of the truck. The driver called back to them, "End of the line. Change cars for God knows where."

The big blond gunner opened the doors at the rear of the truck, pushed them well back against the overhanging bows of a willow, and sprang down. Number Fifteen and Dawson followed, their skin stained sepia, wearing overalls and nondescript felt hats, looking like a pair of Negro laborers after a hard day's work.

The truck had been driven into a thicket alongside a clay surfaced road. In the late afternoon sun, Dawson stared dazedly at the brown flesh of hands and wrists.

"Will this stuff come off?" he asked faintly.

The blond machine gunner laughed. "You get caught in a rain and you'll see how quick it'll come off." He turned abruptly as the gaunt-faced driver of the truck joined them.

"Let's go, boys. This is the spot. A span of mules and an ash wagon, she said." The gaunt man looked at Dawson and, for some reason, laughed. He did something to what Dawson supposed was a hearing aid attached to the front of his blue serge coat, then turned and led them to the road where a tethered mule team was harnessed to a dump-bed wagon.

"Is she close?" Number Fifteen wanted to know.

The driver of the truck nodded. "Her signal is coming in like a house afire." He stood there, staring north along the road for a moment, and then pointed out a gathering cloud of dust that indicated a car traveling at high speed. "Maybe this is Number Three."

Or, Dawson worried, it could be the cops, though if the bridge was blown up, he didn't see how they could have been followed.

The car that approached was a long, low sedan, light gray beneath the brown dust that had settled on it. It slowed, finally stopped abreast the group of men. At the wheel was one of the most beautiful women that Sam Dawson had ever seen.

Her face was a perfect oval, her skin smooth and the hue of old ivory, her eyes green and long. She wore no hat, and her blue-black hair was drawn back from her brow in classic simplicity.

She lowered the window of the car, and her warm mouth smiled at them.

"**I'M AFRAID** I'm lost," she said, her voice smooth, deep. "I'm looking for ten thirty-six Audley Road. Ten—" she paused—"thirty-six."

The gaunt-faced man who wore the hearing air device said, "You're about three miles off the beam, aren't you?"

"Three," she said.

"Ten," he said.

The gunner said, "Thirty-six."

The woman opened the door of the car. "You two come with me." Then, as soon as Numbers Ten and Thirty-six had settled themselves in the wide front seat, the woman leaned forward to address Number Fifteen.

"Any trouble?" she asked. "No opposition from Mr. Zero yet?"

"None here. How about you?"

"No," she replied, sneering at the idea. "I'm beginning to believe Captain Zero is a myth." She accepted a cigarette from the pack the blond gunner proffered, and when she'd lighted it her long green eyes gave Sam Dawson an amused going-over.

"If you're wondering how you're going to get out of Pendleville's guarded boundaries, Mr. Dawson, here's the deal. You're an ash collector."

"I am?" Dawson said, not pleased.

"Number Fifteen will drive the ash wagon up there," she said, "which, unfortunately, doesn't contain any ashes right now. That means you'll have to pick up some, Mr. Dawson, so that it will be thoroughly convincing for you to drive through the police barricade on the other side of town to get to the dumps."

"You mean," Dawson said, "I'm the guy who walks alongside the wagon and lifts ash barrels? Nuh-uh. I never was any good at physical work."

The three other men laughed. The woman didn't. Her eyes became increasingly narrow.

"Listen, Mr. Dawson," she said, "it just might be that you haven't quite got the picture. Why do you suppose it was decided at the last minute that you would be the one to eliminate James Oliver? Because you're such a hot-shot, you think? Let me tell you why it had to be you.

"You were acquitted, weren't you? And no one can be tried twice for the same crime. You came out of that courthouse clean, and just fifteen minutes later you murdered Oliver in front of witnesses. Get the point? Do you think you could beat another murder rap all by yourself?"

Full realization began to dawn on Sam Dawson. Up to now the whole thing had been like some kind of crazy drunken spree, wildly exciting but not altogether real. Now the hangover was beginning to set in.

He was entirely at the mercy of Black Hat's mob. He would do as he was told or the protection of the organization would be withdrawn and he would be left sitting directly on top the electric chair.

The woman glanced down at the diamond-set dial of her tiny wrist watch. Her hand went to the gearshift lever. She directed a scornful glance at Sam Dawson.

40

"So happy ash collecting, Mr. Dawson," she said as the big car rolled smoothly away.

CHAPTER 5
THE ZERO HOUR

LEE ALLYN lay on his back on the narrow hospital cot and thought, They can't do this to me. I've got to get out of here. Right now, I've got to get out.

It was now three minutes past eleven o'clock at night and Allyn had already made two attempts to get into his clothes and leave the room. He realized now that those attempts had been mistakes. Now all the nurses on the floor were aware that they had a problem patient who needed watching.

Aside from being slightly bothered by a lump on the back of his head that had the shape and consistency of a paving brick, he felt fine. He had been feeling fine ever since the end of the evening visiting period when Doro Kelly had left a warm, searching kiss on his lips. Pulse a little rapid, perhaps, but that was all. There was no good reason why he should be confined to the hospital, and he could think of at least a couple of reasons why he should not be.

Doro Kelly had told him that in spite of his heroic efforts the killer, Dawson, had gotten away. And machine gun fire from the getaway vehicle had cut down two of the police department's cycle cops. A bridge had been blown up, effectively blocking the criminals' pursuers and also wrecking Police Chief Ed Cavanaugh's car.

41

"And Cavanaugh?" Allyn had asked. "I suppose he escaped, hale and hearty as ever, perfectly capable of beating my time with you while I lie here and twirl my thumbs, huh?"

The mischievous Kelly smile, at this point, had not helped his condition. She had assured him that Ed Cavanaugh was all right and that she would tell Ed of his concern. And then she'd kissed Allyn, and everything was momentarily rosy.

Now everything was black. There was no privacy in a hospital. Nurses ran in and out of rooms at any and all times, and there was absolutely no guarantee that a nurse or intern wouldn't come popping into his room at midnight. Any nurse who did so would be apt to witness a phenomenon which she would not get over as long as she lived.

Moreover, the nurse would not be inclined to keep his secret, and then where would he be? He'd be a national curiosity, a ward of the state, or maybe the chief attraction of an elaborate freak show. He could lie there on his back and imagine all sorts of unpleasant things that could happen to him if a nurse walked into his room just the right time.

Because at midnight Lee Allyn would disappear.

It wasn't anything that he could do anything about.

As he had tried to explain to Ed Cavanaugh, the only living person who shared his secret, "It's just something that happens periodically. You can set your watch by it. At exactly midnight, I begin to fade out of the picture. I haven't any control over it at all. Some people have headaches every morning. Others have indigestion every night. But I disappear. It's an affliction. Believe me, the first time it happened, I almost lost my mind."

HE WOULD always remember the first time, that unseasonably warm night at the Lockridge Research Foundation near Chicago. While his eye operation had given him vision that was vastly better than the darkness to which he had become accustomed in his youth, his sight still had not measured up to the standards set by the armed services, and in an effort to do something toward the war effort he had offered himself as a human guinea pig for the purposes of medical research.

But there had been many tests. Even now he didn't know which of the radioactive substances, or what combination of them, had been responsible for the phenomenon. But the last experiment to which he had been subjected had amounted to what Dr. Lockridge had expressed as a "terrific jolt of radioactive arsenic" thought to offer curative possibilities in the baffling medical puzzles of leukemia and Hodgkin's disease.

Allyn had gone to sleep in the nude that night, because of the heat. He had awakened an eternity before dawn, had got up to get a drink from the lavatory in the corner of his room. He had taken hold of the glass, was moving it toward the faucet, when he suddenly became aware of something wrong. Moonlight slanting through the window showed him the glass, but where was his hand?

More important, where was Lee Allyn?

He had thought wildly that he was dead, and that this was some vague half-world afterlife. But then, at dawn, he had watched himself gradually gain visual substance until his naked body was as opaque as any naked body.

The next night he did not go to bed at all, but sat, dressed in his pajamas, beside the window. The fear that it might happen again was strong, but stronger still was the fear that it had never actually happened at all—that he was mad.

At midnight the strange metamorphosis began again, the whole process occupying not more than six minutes of time. And then his mirror showed him a pair of cotton pajamas, minus hands, feet, and head. He got up, went to the closet, and began to pull on a pair of wool trousers. It was then he noticed something else unbelievably strange. Where the wool cloth pressed tightly against his body it became translucent at first and then wholly transparent.

Whatever the nature of the rays that emanated from his being, they were selective. The cotton pajamas were not affected, but wool, an animal fiber, was. To become invisible, he had only to strip off all such vegetable-base garments.

WHEN HIS association with the Lockridge Foundation had ended without the doctors discovering his secret, Lee Allyn had at length landed his present job on the Pendleville *World*. He was not considered a brilliant reporter, but he did obtain much inside information which could be put to good use in his midnight-to-dawn rôle as Captain Zero.

His first big investigation had taught the underworld that Captain Zero was a force to be feared, but at the same time Zero had lost the first round in his fight to keep his secret. Ed Cavanaugh, then head of the Pendleville detective bureau, had adroitly pinned the identity of Captain Zero on Lee Allyn. And while Cavanaugh had agreed to keep the secret in exchange for close cooperation, Lee Allyn's greatest fear remained with him always—that the day might come when he would be revealed as a freak of the atomic age.

It was little wonder that he could not rest that night in the Pendleville hospital, practically under the nose of an over-zealous nurse, with the zero hour of midnight swiftly approaching.

During the past hour he had made three quick trips

Doro Kelly

to the closet of his room and back to the cot again, each time gaining some appurtenance essential to his rôle as Captain Zero. His first move had been to replace horn-rimmed glasses with contact lenses.

On his next trip to the closet he had put on tight-fitting trunks and T-shirt knitted from fine, white wool yarn. He had just slipped back into the cotton hospital gown when a couple of nurses picked that portion of the hall directly in front of his door to discuss plans for a Sunday afternoon double date. One of them noticed Allyn moving about in the semi-darkness within his room.

"You get back into bed, you!" she ordered.

So he got back into bed. It was then fifteen minutes before midnight. He silently cursed the report that there was a shortage of nurses when there were obviously too damned many. He held up a hand, fingers widely spread and studied the natural aura of pink translucency outlining the bones of his fingers.

Twelve minutes. Ten, and out in the hall one of the nurses said, "There's a light on fourteen. You take it, Grace."

Dammit, both of you take it! Lee Allyn thought desperately, and then saw the two girls disappear in opposite directions along the hall. Allyn kicked down the sheet and crossed to the closet again, this time to get the special footgear he always carried in the pocket of his suit coat—a pair of woolen socks to which he had sewed a thin, tough sole of rawhide, an animal fiber readily reduced to transparency by the strange invisible rays which would soon begin to emanate from every portion of his body.

Brisk footsteps came along the hall then, and Allyn turned quickly. The room kept turning after he'd stopped, swimming dizzily. He lurched back toward the cot, struck the table beside it thigh high, grabbed and saved the water pitcher which clattered against its tray and made a hell of a noise. He dived in under the bed-sheet just as the floor nurse came through the door and approached the cot.

"Why aren't you asleep?" she demanded.

He glared at her. "I am. Why don't you go away?"

She sat down in the chair beside the cot, took hold of his right wrist. She looked at her watch, and so did he. *Her* watch said about half a minute before midnight.

He thought, Good lord, if it begins to happen while she's holding my hand, if my fingers start to disappear—

He jerked his hand away from her and shoved it under the sheet. He looked at her, his eyes wild.

"What's the matter with you?" she asked crossly. "You've got a pulse like a rivet hammer."

"It's love," he said bitterly. "The touch of your hand starts my heart to bouncing around."

"Phooie!" she said and got up to look at the chart at the foot of his cot. She nodded conclusively. "I'm going to fix you, Mr. Allyn. Just as soon as I can get back from the dispensary, I'm going to fix you." She turned with an angry rustle of her starched uniform and left the room.

Allyn kicked out from under the sheets and sat up on the edge of the bed. He held a hand to the light, noticed that the natural aura had become less pink, was gradually fading until the dark shadows that were fingerbones became as distinct as though he had placed his hand above a fluoroscope. Next the shadows would thin, fade utterly.

HE YANKED the wool, rawhide-soled socks onto feet he could scarcely see, stood, got out of the cotton hospital gown. How long would it take for the nurse to get the hypo from the dispensary? Five minutes? Not less than that. It musn't take less than that!

Swiftly now his undistinguished face became the merest shadow of itself, the bones of the skull clearly defined at first and then fading to a light gray, blurring out of the picture; the gray mass that was his brain, blurring out of the picture. Arms and legs had already dissolved to complete transparency.

And now a pair of trunks and a T-shirt, seemingly suspended

in midair and faintly luminous, melted entirely from view as the invisible rays flowed through each cell of the animal fibers. There was nothing left to mark his location in the room except his wrist watch, and he took that off, moved to the closet.

He put his watch into a pocket of his suit coat along with the case that contained his glasses. He took all of his clothes from the closet and hastily made a bundle of them, coat on the outside, buttoned, the sleeves tied. He snapped out the light.

Had any of the nurses entered his room then they would have seen a bundle of clothing apparently floating across the little room to the window, would have seen the sash lift of its own volition. The invisible Captain Zero thrust Lee Allyn's clothing through the window, let them fall two stories to land somewhere near one of the rear entrances of the hospital. Zero got the sash down as far as the top of the glass draft deflector and then twisted around, alarmed by approaching footsteps. The nurse was back, carrying a tray on which was a small glass containing some colorless fluid and a hypodermic needle.

"Now, Mr. Allyn—" She broke off as her eyes moved from the tray in her hand to the empty cot.

CHAPTER 6
THE PHANTOM SIGN

THE NURSE hurriedly put the tray down on the table. Lips thinned in exasperation, she turned to the closet, opened it, found Allyn's clothing gone.

"Damn that little man!" she said and went out into the corridor.

The little man who wasn't there was right behind her. When she turned to address another nurse who had come out of a room three doors down the hall she was looking right through Captain Zero.

"Browning, he's gone!" the floor nurse jerked her head to indicate Lee Allyn's room.

"Gone?" Nurse Browning repeated bewilderedly. "How could he be? I've been right here in the hall except for the second I stepped into Room Twelve."

"Then he couldn't have gone far. Try the stairs. I'll 'phone the front office to head him off."

Nurse Browning ran toward the stairway with Zero trotting silently along beside her. She opened a door, which was kind of her inasmuch as the door was largely composed of glass and it was therefore impossible for Zero to open it without announcing his presence to any chance onlooker. He and the nurse went down the flight of stairs together and then separated at the first floor where Zero descended six steps to an outer door. He had to get his clothes, even though they were now more of a hindrance than a help to him.

He had to get them because if he didn't and they were found, the alarm would be spread that Lee Allyn had slipped out of the hospital in the nude. Since this was hardly possible without attracting a good dead of attention, the whole uncomfortable situation might suggest to somebody that Lee Allyn and Captain Zero were one and the same person.

He hesitated a moment in front of the door, glanced back to make sure that there was no one watching, then pushed the door open. He stopped, the door and his mouth agape. Just beyond was a crushed-stone parking lot. Not ten feet from him, in the full illumination of a powerful light above the doorway, he saw his clothing. He heaved the clothing into a foundation planting of junipers that brushed his legs, slowed down as he neared the lighted area at the front of the hospital, finally stopped. Then he went diagonally across the parking lot.

He heaved a sigh, stepped out into the light, followed the sidewalk around in front of the building, and turned toward the street. There was only one other person on the approach walk—a tall man wearing a gray suit and hat, his rugged face all planes and angles as though it had been carved laboriously from some dark wood.

Zero waited until the other was unknowingly abreast of him and then he addressed Pendleville's chief of police, Ed Cavanaugh.

"Cavanaugh." This time it was the deep, quiet yet strangely resonant voice of Captain Zero.

ED CAVANAUGH didn't appear in the least startled. He paused, fumbled in his pocket, brought out a cigarette which he placed between thin lips. Mouth hidden by hands that cupped a lighted match, he whispered:

"I got to wondering what you'd do when midnight rolled around. I started to worry."

"That makes two of us," Zero returned. *"Get my clothes will you,*

Cavanaugh? In those junipers on the south side of the building. Can you give me a lift?"

"I can. In fact, I've got to talk to you." Cavanaugh flipped the burned match away and moved on up the approach walk. Zero went out to the street to find a police department car at the curb. Presently the police chief was returning with the bundle of Lee Allyn's clothes tucked under his arm.

"Are you around here somewhere?" Cavanaugh said in a whisper.

"Right beside you," Zero replied.

Cavanaugh laughed dryly. "Sometime somebody's going to accuse me of talking to myself." He opened the front door, got in, gave the invisible Zero a chance to join him on the seat cushions before closing the door.

"Anything new since the massacre downtown this afternoon?" Zero asked as soon as Ed Cavanaugh had the car under way.

"That's a good word for it—massacre," the chief said grimly, "They got Griffeth and Weihunt with their damned machine gun, two of the best cops we've got. And James Oliver, of course. He didn't have a chance. The gun Dawson used was small calibre, but somebody had drilled holes into the noses of the slugs— made dum-dums out of them. They spattered. There's no ballistics evidence to go on at all."

"Then you don't know where Dawson got the gun?"

"We don't know where the gun came from originally, if that's what you mean. But it was passed to him in a newspaper he bought on the courthouse steps, and—" Cavanaugh broke off as the invisible man beside him swore softly, "What's the matter?"

"I had a sneaking suspicion that newshawk wasn't Ben Keeler."

"It wasn't. We checked, of course, and Ben Keeler has been in bed with a cold for three days."

"Then if I'd followed through on my hunch instead of playing hero we might have had at least one member of the gang behind bars."

"I doubt it," Cavanaugh said. "The lad posing as Ben Keeler would have polished you off at the same time Dawson was taking care of Oliver. You did all right, and you're plenty lucky to get out with nothing more than a headache. Whatever this mob is up to is something big—big enough for them to take any sort of risk and kill anybody who gets in their way."

Zero was thoughtfully silent a moment.

"You knew, didn't you, that Arthur Henshaw showed up at the Dawson trial?"

"Henshaw?" Cavanaugh didn't remember the name.

"The salesman from Indianapolis I told you about. He checked out of a sample room in the local hotel before he had a chance to sell anything right after the McClaren girl was killed. I tackled him in Indianapolis. I still think he knew something about the McClaren girl's murder."

"So what?" Cavanaugh interrupted. "That's all water under the bridge. We could have had ten witnesses and the best we would have got was a hung jury. Some money changed hands somewhere—some pretty filthy lucre. My guess is that James Oliver was the boy who had his hand out."

Zero stared straight ahead at the cold blue lights in front of the police headquarters building some blocks distant.

"Look, Cavanaugh," he said. *"If Oliver was bribed to stick for a*

verdict of not guilty, then you're concluding that Oliver was killed to stop any investigation on that bribery angle—right?"

"Right."

"Now hang onto that for a second and recall who killed Oliver. Mr. Sam Dawson. Also right? So somebody paid out money to buy a juror to free Dawson and then had Dawson kill the juror in front of plenty of witnesses, putting Dawson right where he was in the first place—behind the eight ball, guilty of a second first degree murder."

"Uh—not quite," Cavanaugh said, his voice dropping to a whisper as he put the car into the stall reserved for it at the side of the police building. "There's a slight difference there which is one of the things I'd like to talk to you about. Come on."

CAVANAUGH SLID out from under the wheel, did not close the car door until he had given Captain Zero ample time to alight. Then the police chief led the way into the building by a side door, up a short flight of steps, and into his office. When he had closed the door and hung up his hat, he said:

"Sit down somewhere."

"I am sitting down," Zero's voice came from one of the oak chairs beside the chief's desk.

Cavanaugh stared somewhat uneasily at that particular chair as he got around to his own behind the desk.

Zero said, *"If you'd get softer chairs in here, I'd show."*

"You'll show if you smoke a cigarette, won't you?" Cavanaugh said gruffly, proffering his package.

"Uh-huh, if I inhale."

"Then inhale, because I don't care too much about talking to a man I can't see." Cavanaugh pulled out his swivel chair and

53

sat down, watched fascinated while unseen hands struck flame from a desk lighter and carried it to the tip of a cigarette that appeared suspended in space.

"You were going to point out that there was an all-important difference between Sam Dawson's current status and what it was when he faced trial in our court of justice," Zero reminded the police chief.

"Well, the difference is this," Cavanaugh lighted his own cigarette. "Now Dawson is at liberty. He wasn't before, remember?"

"But he's guilty of a second killing—"

"Wait a minute now," Cavanaugh held up his hand. His smile was thin. "You're being absolutely logical. I admit that the thing looks as though it went around in a circle, just as you say. It *looks* that way. It did to me until I began to recall that within the past eight months there have been exactly ten beautiful engineered prison breaks at different parts of the country. Some of our most notorious criminals are now on the loose.

" 'Bugs' Barton from Alcatraz, Ned 'The Chill' Childers from San Quentin, to name a couple. Barton and Childers are both guilty of the crimes for which they were sentenced as well as the new charges for breaking prison. But the point is—" and Cavanaugh stared fixedly at the red mote of Zero's cigarette—"that Childers and Barton *and* our own Sam Dawson are all at liberty."

The chief leaned back in the swivel chair and raked his fingers through mahogany-colored hair. "Think that over a minute. See if you come up with the same conclusion I did."

Zero drew thoughtfully on his cigarette. *"You mean you*

think the same brain engineered these prison breaks that managed Dawson's getaway?"

Cavanaugh was nodding.

"Then the only possible conclusion that I can see," Zero continued, *"is that whatever happens to an individual like Dawson doesn't particularly matter to the brain behind the scheme. That is, it doesn't matter that Dawson is guilty as charged, it only matters that he is at liberty and of use to the somebody who is responsible for his being at liberty."*

"That's it exactly." Cavanaugh banged forward in his chair, and the finger he pointed for emphasis trembled slightly. This is something bigger than Bugs Barton, Chill Childers, or Sam Dawson, as individuals. And I wish to God I knew what's at the core of it." For a moment he stared through Zero and at the wall. Then he added moodily, "I don't suppose there's anything much to do except keep pecking away at the edges and see what we can find."

"What have you got at the edges?" Zero asked.

"The usual assortment of descriptions you get from a panicky bunch of witnesses to a shooting. Only one point of agreement there. Three persons who saw the getaway truck say that the driver wore a hearing aid. So we're looking twice at all deaf men.

"Incidentally we found the truck abandoned just off Audley Road. It was well protected with an armor plate lining. There was a paint spray inside containing some water soluble brown stuff, and this seems to tie with a couple of supposed Negro trash collectors who got through the police barricade shortly after dusk and deserted their mule team south of town."

ZERO WHISTLED softly. *"That's neat."*

"Yeah, damned if it isn't," Cavanaugh agreed dryly. "Working at the thing from another angle, I've talked to James Oliver's widow. If I'd been playing dominoes I couldn't have drawn more blanks."

"He was a lady-chaser, wasn't he?"

"Maybe. Mrs. Oliver isn't talking. If you can shake her loose from whatever she's hiding, I'd surely appreciate it."

"I'll give it a whirl," Zero promised. *"Tonight."*

"Wait a minute." Cavanaugh looked about rather sheepishly. "That is, if you've started to go anywhere."

"I haven't."

Cavanaugh opened the top drawer of his desk and brought out a folded newspaper, a Home Edition of the *World,* which he spread out.

"This was clutched in your hot little hand when they scraped you up off the sidewalk and shipped you to the hospital. Apparently you grabbed it from Dawson when you and he went down together. Remember?"

"Vaguely."

"Those oil spots came from the gun that was wrapped in it," Cavanaugh explained. "The gun that got Oliver. But what do you think of that?" His finger pointed to the margin above the headline of the story about the Dawson trial. There, hand-lettered in pencil was:

KILL ØLIVER IMMEDIATELY

Zero said, " *'Complete instructions packed with every weapon,'* huh? *What's the mark through the 'O' in the 'Oliver?'* "

"I'm getting some screwy answers to that."

"Such as?"

"That the circle with a line drawn through it like that is a code sign universally recognized by hobos."

"Enlighten me," Zero said. *"What kind of a sign?"*

"It sometimes shows up on sidewalks or fences and indicates that the house so marked is easily robbed."

"Got anything better than that? I somehow haven't received the impression that we're up against a group of knights of the road and rattler."

Cavanaugh shrugged. "I said they were screwy answers, didn't I? Our mutual friend Doro Kelly likes the idea that it's a Greek letter."

"She means 'Phi' like in Phi Beta Kappa, huh?"

"Yeah. She's already given the criminals the label 'Phi Gang' in the story she's doing for your paper. She claims it's a kind of secret signature without which no such death warrant is genuine."

"Hm," Zero mused. *"Well, could be. How many wise guys have told you that if you mark the 'O' in 'Oliver' all you've got is the 'liver?'* "

"Enough so that I swore I'd kill the next one who made that crack," Cavanaugh replied, "but I'll make an exception of you. Are you leaving now?"

"I think I'd better. It's close to one A.M. by your clock there. I don't want to make Mrs. Oliver lose any more sleep than I have to."

Cavanaugh sighed enviously. "You know that must be pretty damned nice to be able to slip in and out of most any place without anybody knowing you're around."

Zero's laugh was short and bitter. *"Yeah, you should try it, pal. You'd slip in a lot of places, wouldn't you? You'd travel light, too—no gun, no money, no watch, no anything but just little old you. And you can't imagine the fun you'd have trying to board a bus or flag down a taxi."*

Cavanaugh hadn't thought of that. He now looked at that portion of the air which he thought represented Captain Zero with new respect.

"How about a lift out to the Oliver place? It's on the river, a good two miles from here."

"If you'll clear out and let me have a free hand with Mrs. Oliver," was Zero's ungracious acceptance. He was reminded by the chief's thoughtless envy that invisibility all too frequently assumed the proportions of a liability rather than an asset.

"I'll take you out there and drop you," Cavanaugh promised, getting out of his chair. "And then you're on your own."

CHAPTER 7
WIDOW OF A DEAD WOLF

THE RIVER at flood stage washed the foot of the steep slope behind the sprawled ranch-type house, and Edith Oliver listened to its constant voice. It was to be company for her in this, her first night of utter loneliness. She stared at the window, awash with moonlight, and listened to the river, and remembered other wakeful nights when she had sat in the darkness of the bedroom alone, tormented by jealous speculation.

But he had always come back to her.

Now he would not come back. Now he was dead, and she knew why he was dead. Had she been less inclined to let him shape his destiny separately from hers, she might have told James Oliver that some day something like this would happen.

She got up from the boudoir chair, crossed to the door, went into the hall and then into the living room. She would warm a glass of milk, perhaps put a little rum and honey into it, and if she drank that she might be able to get some sleep. She had turned on the living-room light, had started for the kitchen when the front chime sounded.

She stopped, glancing at the clock. A telegram, she supposed, from his people or from hers. Perhaps the shock of hearing of her son's death had brought on one of Mother Oliver's heart attacks. She hoped it wasn't that. Tightening the sash of her white satin robe, she hurried to the door, turned on the entry light.

She got the door open, but there was no one there. A physically strong, nerveless woman, she stepped across the threshold and looked along the street. A pair of red tail lamps winked at her from a car that was accelerating toward the corner, and she came to a logical conclusion, as she usually did: someone had got the wrong address, had discovered the mistake, had left in a tremendous hurry.

Yet had there been time for that in the interval between the ringing of the bell and her opening of the door? She thought not, wondered about it a little as she stepped back into the house and closed and locked the door. Her mind moved ahead of her toward the kitchen, warm milk with rum in it, and sleep. That was pleasant to think upon.

"Thank you, Mrs. Oliver."

Edith Oliver stopped halfway across the living room. Her breathing stopped too. She turned slowly, her brown eyes motionless in her thin, appealing face, dry lips just apart.

There was no one, yet she had heard a voice. A deep and quiet voice, compelling, not unpleasant, and very real.

"Captain Zero," it spoke now with a slight apologetic note, from about six feet in front of her. *"Don't be frightened, Mrs. Oliver. I won't bother you any longer than I have to. But—"* now with determination—*"for just as long as I have to."*

SHE HAD read of Captain Zero and had assigned him to that imaginative realm whence came flying disks and sea monsters and other doubtful fantasies. But now, hearing his voice, seeing two tiny pin-points of reflected light which she logically assumed might represent his eyes, her sober judgment told her to believe in him.

"Yes?" She took a shallow breath. "What do you want?"

"Sit down," Zero urged gently. *"Please."* He watched her move to a Lawson sofa and sit down on the edge of it. It was a relief to him to find a woman who did not faint, or scream, or assume that he was a hallucination brought on by too much drinking. He liked her calm good looks, her poise, and he wondered how James Oliver had failed to appreciate her.

"What do you want?" she persisted coolly, and he crossed to an upholstered chair in which he sat so that she could see the outline of his substance impressed upon the cushions. This bewildered her a little. She closed her eyes, then slowly opened them.

His gentle laugh was intended to assume her. *"Some information about Mr. Oliver. About his—murder."*

Her eyes didn't flinch but there was a stiffening about her mouth, and Zero knew what Cavanaugh had been up against— the adamant quality of her resistance. Well, he had to break that down somehow, to crack the shell.

She was saying, "I have no information. Had I any I would have given it to the police."

"I see." As though he intended to accept that as final. He sat there a moment, and then he continued. *"Two months ago,"* he told her, *"a notorious criminal by the name of Bugs Barton escaped from Alcatraz. He didn't escape by himself. It was a beautifully planned prison break, executed with split-second timing."*

Her eyes stared at the chair in which he sat, trying to fathom his line of approach.

"Three weeks before that, at San Quentin, there was another perfectly engineered prison break. A man by the name of Childers got out. Childers, nicknamed 'the Chill'—guess why? Because he's adept at chilling people. With a gun. If we don't think about these events, they don't bother us.

"But then if we do think about them—" there was a deadly seriousness in his voice now—*"if we add Alcatraz to San Quentin to Pendleville to nine or ten other similar jobs, if we stop to realize that all of these schemes were hatched in the same brain, the enormity of the plan becomes a little frightening, doesn't it?"*

"What plan?"

Zero replied frankly, *"I don't know. I don't know anything further than that someone is developing an organization of the most ruthless criminals of our time."*

Edith Oliver's face flushed. "I—I don't believe it."

"You don't believe what?"

"That—that my husband's murder had anything to do with a nation-wide plot."

"It didn't," he said mildly. *"My point exactly. A mere incident. He wasn't even in the way of the criminal machine. He was only in a position where he might, at some future time, have got in its way. It doesn't matter if we ignore it all now, because if we just sit and wait long enough the master-mind behind it all will pull his coup. And then we'll know."*

EDITH OLIVER took a tremulous breath. "You win. I'll tell you what I know, Captain Zero. But believe me, I didn't realize it was anything like this. I'm still not wholly convinced. I—I thought—well, I thought that James had been poaching on some gangster's domain.

"He'd been playing around with a woman, and I thought, after yesterday's shooting, that some mob chief had considered that woman his own particular property. Here is all I know, and when I am through I leave the rest entirety up to you."

He waited patiently for a moment while Edith Oliver organized her story.

"My father is a minister," she began, "which may explain why I have always looked with abhorrence upon divorce. I have known for years that I was not the only woman in my husband's life, for he never bothered particularly with concealment and sometimes even bragged to me about his escapades.

"But last week an incident occurred which changed my outlook entirely. I was at home, alone as usual, suffering from a severe headache. Unable to find any aspirin in the house, I got into my car and went to the drugstore. The neighborhood stores were all closed and I had to go all the way downtown. And there, on the street, I came face to face with my husband in the company of a woman.

"I don't know that he saw me. He probably didn't. He was enjoying himself so completely that he wouldn't have noticed me even if I had addressed him by name."

"The woman," Zero interrupted. *"What did she look like?"*

"She was the most perfect combination of beauty and evil that I have ever seen. Tall, perfectly proportioned, with an oval face the shade of old ivory. Her hair was blue-black and straight, drawn back from her brow and worn in a soft bun at the nape of her neck. Her eyes were long, narrow, somewhat tilted at the outer extremities, and they were as green as jade, indescribably evil. I somehow got the impression that the eyes were the real woman, the face a kind of mask."

Zero drew a long breath. *"I've seen her,"* he said. In Indianapolis, he had seen her, in the company of Arthur Henshaw. *"I believe her name is Maria Renard. One of her names, at any rate. What did you do, Mrs. Oliver?"*

The woman shook her head. "Nothing. I went back to my car, and when they came out of the tavern an hour later, I followed them to her place."

63

"The address," Zero prompted, trying to conceal his excitement. This was the first chink in the periphery of the thing, the first defect in the wall of secrecy that surrounded the master blueprint. A woman had been behind James Oliver's culpability as a juror. Her name was Maria Renard. If Zero could reach her—

"The address was 265 Hathorn Street," Mrs. Oliver told him.

The door chime sounded. Edith Oliver started to get up, then glanced at the chair which Zero had occupied. The hollows in the cushions were slowly filling. Her eyes sprang down to the soft carpet, saw his footprints progress to the door.

"Who—who is it?" she whispered.

"Hush." Zero was peering out through the small pane of glass set in the upper panel of the door. On the step outside stood the gaunt figure of a man wearing a blue serge suit and a gray hat pulled low over his eyes. Of the face Zero could see nothing from this angle except the lean jaw and the left ear. A black cord or wire dangled from something behind that ear, down to a flat black plastic case fastened to the front of his coat. A hearing aid.

The driver of the getaway truck had been a deaf man, too!

The gaunt man touched the button of the door chime again.

"Turn out the light," Zero whispered.

"But—"

"Do as I say. Turn out the light in here, leave the one outside going. When you open the door, do it fast and keep clear of the opening."

EDITH OLIVER moved to the wall switch. He heard her say with a trace of bitterness, "Another—incident?"

He didn't know, but he wasn't taking any chances. The man

outside the door was tapping his foot impatiently, whistling tunelessly as anybody might while waiting for someone to open the door. But he wore a hearing aid.

Edith Oliver brushed past Captain Zero in the dark, uttered a small, startled sound as she touched his unseen body.

"Quickly," he reminded her. *"And keep clear of the doorway."*

The doorknob rattled in her nervous grasp. She turned, drew an audible breath, and yanked the door open.

The gaunt face lifted, plainly visible in the light outside. Eyes set in deep pits that looked as though they were smudged with charcoal quickly flicked into the gloomy interior of the living room.

"I hate to disturb you at this hour," the man said hoarsely, "but I'm from the police department." He stepped across the sill, and his right hand moved casually toward the side pocket of his suit coat.

Zero caught the man's wrist. At the same time, Zero's left arm came up, streaked in a short arc, the edge of his rigidly open hand connecting with the back of the man's neck. The man collapsed like a puppet clipped from its strings. Zero dragged him forward far enough so that the door could be closed.

"Hold it a minute," he cautioned Edith Oliver as he heard her running toward the light switch. *"No lights yet. Not until we see what we've got."*

She uttered strained laughter at the paradox of seeing in the dark. She could not have known, of course, that once upon a time there had been a blind boy named Lee Allyn who had been compelled to develop his tactual sense to the nth degree.

"He—he really isn't from the police, is he, Mr. Zero?" the woman whispered.

"Hardly." Zero had pulled the man's gun—an automatic rather than a police revolver. He straightened, listening. Footsteps were pelting along the side of the house. There was a whistle, a thin, sustained note, not loud but penetrating.

"What was that?" Mrs. Oliver stammered out.

A signal, he thought. He said, *"You'd better get to the 'phone and call the police."*

"What are you going to do?" She was moving across the room to the 'phone.

He didn't know what he was going to do, but he wished he hadn't insisted on playing this one alone. The man at his feet wasn't the only one in on this caper. This mob left nothing to chance. They were after Mrs. Oliver because they knew she had connected the green-eyed Maria Renard with James Oliver.

From somewhere in the rear of the house came the crash and shatter of breaking glass. Then Edith Oliver screamed.

So now they were coming in.

"The guest closet over there—get into it! And stay there."

He heard the closet door close. He stooped over the unconscious man, hoisted him like a shield, moved to the swinging door at the end of the room. At the door he stopped, the other man balanced in front of him, his weight hanging on Zero's invisible arms. Zero put out his left foot suddenly, swung the door open. A knee kick bounced the unconscious man through the door and into the kitchen.

Nothing happened. The man fell on his face and lay still.

Zero's eyes moved to the back door which possibly opened on a patio. Glass in this door had been broken, a shard of it still remaining in the frame, catching a glint of moonlight.

Silence pressed down upon the house. He didn't like it—that heavy, brooding kind of silence. He moved into the kitchen, an L-shaped room with a breakfast alcove, and it was there that he found another door leading into one of the wings.

SOMEONE BEHIND the door uttered a dry cough. That was all—no footsteps—just the cough. A come-on maybe, Zero thought. All right. If it had to come sometime, it might as well come now. He raised the automatic. His left hand on the doorknob was steady. He turned the knob over, pushed back the door.

The blinding ray of an electric torch struck across his face, and he fired twice in panic. The light was gone. There was an explosive hiss of sound as though one of his slugs might have punctured a steam boiler. Something like cold rain drenched his extended right arm to the shoulder.

He jerked back and slammed the door, stared at the arm and hand in front of him. His own hand, his own arm, no longer invisible, but bathed in some sort of luminous paint that dripped like liquid moonlight from his fist and elbow.

Behind the door, somebody said, "Come on in after me, Mr. Zero."

From the front part of the house came shot after shot in such rapid succession that the crashes were welded into a single continuous roar. Above all that, he heard the agonized scream of Edith Oliver.

Zero whirled and sprang across the kitchen, racing back the

way he had come, no longer cautious and sure-footed but stumbling in his haste. Lights burned in the living room. The air was acrid with cordite fumes, the gunsmoke swirling about.

His gaze jerked toward the closet, its door still closed, the panel riddled with bullet holes. And down at the bottom, blood seeped out from under the edge and across the floor.

How had they known that Mrs. Oliver was in that closet? There had been no time for trial-and-error fumbling. One of the gang had entered the living room—probably from the bedroom wing—and had simply poured lead into the closet without even bothering to open the door.

Zero opened the door. She'd fallen against it, her back to it, and now her torso tipped limply backward onto the carpet at his feet. He saw the glazed eyes, the open mouth with its blood-flecked lips. A faint creak of sound, which he placed at the swinging door of the kitchen, brought him sharply around.

He fired at the swinging door, and as he bounded to the sill of the open front door, lead plowed into the woodwork next to the visible right arm of his. Outside it was more of the same, from a different source—the crash of gunfire from the south end of the house.

Zero dived into rank grown shrubbery beside the door, went plowing through to the opposite corner, ducked around it, pausing in his headlong flight long enough for a snap shot at a man who came into the area of light before the front door. The man stumbled and fell.

Zero ran to the back of the house. The man who was still inside the house pumped lead through the broken glass of the back door, his target for tonight that single visible and luminous arm of Captain Zero. Zero zigzagged down the steep slope toward the river, fell over something, finally rolled down the bank and splashed into the water. He came up spluttering in the shallows, and the hell-hounds were still on his heels. He saw them at the top of the bank—two men still, two guns streaking the dark with orange-yellow flame. And far and away the squall of police sirens rode the night air.

Zero frog-leaped out of the shallows as far out into the boisterous flood waters as possible. Some black and shapeless hulk of flotsam came bearing down upon him. He dove under it, surfaced on the other side, clung to its edge with chilled fingertips.

Gasping, he let the swift current carry him on….

CHAPTER 8
TOO MANY DEAD MEN

I T WASN'T until after eight that Lee Allyn was awakened by Mrs. Parsley's woodpecker tapping on his door.

"Mr. Allyn, you got comp'ny down in the parlor."

He groaned. "Tell 'em I don't want any."

Mrs. Parsley uttered a giggle that was a bit malicious. "You really want me to?"

"That's what I said."

"All righty, Mr. Allyn, I'll just do that. I'll just trot down those stairs as fast as shank's mare will take me and tell Miss Kelly you don't want any!"

"Huh?" He struggled up from the bed. "Hey, now wait a minute! You tell Miss Kelly I'll be right down."

"I thought that would change your mind," Mrs. Parsley chuckled and went off down the stairs.

He got up, found that Ed Cavanaugh had thoughtfully delivered his clothing and had even gone so far as to put the suit on a hanger in the closet. Allyn put on his robe, went down the hall to the bath where he showered and shaved. He returned to his room, and dressed.

In the parlor sat Doro Kelly looking prettier than any woman ought to have looked at this hour of the morning, in her trim black suit and jaunty black beret that made the blue of her eyes an inky blue. She stood and struck a severe arms-akimbo attitude that was not too convincing.

"What's the big idea, Lee Allyn, of ducking out of the hospital when you were under doctors' orders to stay there and get two days of rest?"

"Well, it's like this," he explained lightly. "Our hospital is not staffed with the sort of nurses Hollywood has led the male patient to expect. Long on efficiency, they were remarkably short on pulchritude. Nobody mothered me—just kicked me around. See?"

She kept looking at him, narrow-eyed, suspicious.

"Anyway," he said, "I got a lead on a story. Mystery woman enters Dawson case—how's that for a streamer?"

The Kelly nose crinkled. "Not today. You might head a column with it, but today's streamer will have to do with Mrs. Oliver's bullet-riddled body."

70

His small face went blank. "How's that?" he asked and for the next few minutes listened to a rehash of the murder of Edith Oliver. Doro was able to add only one significant thing to what he already knew: the police had failed to nail a single member of the gang.

"Well now," he said when she had finished, "my mystery woman story ought to make a follow-up. That is, if we can get anything on it."

"Where do we go?" Doro Kelly wanted to know as they went out into the fresh spring morning and got in her Plymouth coupé.

"We go to 265 Hathorn," he told Doro as she poked at the starter, "where we ask for one Maria Renard."

"The mystery woman?" Doro meshed gears, let the clutch in smoothly.

"Right. A lady very palsy with James Oliver before the Dawson trial. She is also palsy with a party by the name of Arthur Henshaw, wholesale drygoods merchant working out of Indianapolis."

"So what?"

"So, Arthur Henshaw attends the Dawson trial, and when he hears Hattie McClaren's mother bewail the blind lurching course of justice, Mr. Arthur Henshaw promptly faints and falls down stairs. It is also interesting to recall that, the night of the murder, Henshaw leaves Pendleville for Indianapolis under rather peculiar circumstances.

"That is, after engaging a sample room the previous evening, he checks out at around four in the morning, shortly after the

McClaren girl was knifed, without waiting for the business day to dawn."

"And this Henshaw is a friend of Maria Renard," Doro said. "And so was James Oliver. Both are associated in some remote fashion with the Dawson trial, and the whole thing goes around and around and doesn't necessarily arrive anywhere."

"That's right," he agreed, suddenly grave. "It's all periphery. And as Ed Cavanaugh says, all we're doing is pecking at the edges."

DORO DROVE on for a moment in silence and then said, "Did Cavanaugh show you the newspaper you snatched out of Sam Dawson's hand yesterday afternoon?"

He nodded.

"What do you make of it?"

"The sign, you mean—the thing you're calling *phi?* I can't figure it all out."

"What do you make of any part of it?"

His small face crinkled in a frown of perplexity. "I don't know. It doesn't seem to fit."

"What do you mean?"

"Well, we've got a killing followed by a perfectly planned getaway including an armored truck, a machine gun barrage for cover, a mined bridge, a lightning makeup job that enables two men to slip through police lines disguised as trash collectors. We've got all that and then a rather crude, hand-lettered message of instruction given to Sam Dawson."

"Simple, direct, and to the point."

"Too simple, too direct," he argued. "And it doesn't fit. If he'd received his instruction in code flashed from an electric sign or something like that, I'd say that fitted. This other doesn't. We're either missing the most significant thing about it, or it's a red herring."

"Red herring, my left ankle!"

"You mean your pretty left ankle."

"The message was delivered to Dawson. It said kill Oliver. Dawson killed Oliver, and you sit there and try to tell me it's a red herring. If it is, my name is Jankowski!"

Her name was obviously Kelly, and her Irish showed, and he thought she was never prettier than when she was flushed and angry. He said nothing but eyed her and swallowed past the lump that formed in his throat as he thought of the insurmountable barrier between them.

Her infatuation with Captain Zero was no comfort to him. How could romance come between a perfectly normal woman and a man who was invisible forever, especially when that invisible man was, during daylight hours, a rather insignificant person whom Doro tolerated but whom she probably never thought of marrying.

He felt reasonably sure that the only thing that kept her from marrying Ed Cavanaugh was this illusion she had regarding Captain Zero—an illusion that would probably be smashed if she ever learned the true identity of Zero.

They had come now into Hathorn Street, in the old but substantial west side of town. Number 265 was in the middle of a block of unimaginative brick houses, differing from the others in that it had a sign on the porch rail that read:

LIGHT HOUSEKEEPING ROOMS

"Not my idea of the proper setting for a mystery woman," Doro said as she set the handbrake and flipped off the ignition.

"You can't tell from here," Allyn said. "The lady could be standing hip-deep in white fur rugs right now and you couldn't tell from here." He got out, hurried around the car with the idea of assisting Doro, but she had already alighted.

THEY WENT up onto a wide porch and knocked at a door. The woman who answered was a short, motherly person of about sixty wearing a blue kitchen apron over a blue housedress. Her smile was pleasant, and before they could say anything she came to some definite conclusions.

"Oh, you want to see the room, don't you? It's such a perfect place for young married folk to start out in."

"That's a good idea—" Allyn began.

"But we're not married," Doro concluded for him, and she looked at him as though she didn't think it was an especially good idea.

"Oh," said the woman. "Oh my! I've put my foot in it again. Davie always says I never open my mouth but what I put my foot in it. But what can I do for you, then?"

"We're looking for one of your tenants, a Miss Renard," Allyn said.

"Miss Renard?" the landlady repeated, frowning. "No one by that name here. Are you sure you have the right address? Or maybe you mean Miss Bernardo. I have a Miss Bernardo."

"Tall?" Allyn said. "Blue-black hair, long green eyes?" The woman was shaking her head.

"You mean Mrs. Volsanger," the landlady informed him.

"Why, yes!" Allyn pounced on the name. He nudged Doro. "Didn't she marry someone by the name of Volsanger?"

Doro nodded. "Vol—something, it was. A queer name, I do remember that."

The landlady was smiling and nodding her gray head. "You're friends of Mrs. Volsanger?"

"Oh, yes."

"Charming person, isn't she?" the landlady cooed. "So lovely to look at and such a wonderful personality. Isn't it a shame that she's deaf?"

"Huh?" Lee Allyn's mouth fell open, and Doro closed it for him with a kick in the shin.

"Yes, it is," Doro said. "She's so young."

"But nobody would know it, I don't suppose," the landlady prattled on. "These new hearing aids are so deceptive nowadays. I wouldn't have even guessed it if I hadn't seen the gadget on her dresser one day last week. The little dingus—you know—" she pulled at an earlobe—"you couldn't tell it from an earring."

"Can we see her?" Allyn asked. "If she isn't up we'd be glad to wait."

The landlady blinked at him in surprise. "Oh, didn't I tell you? Mrs. Volsanger moved out yesterday noon."

Allyn and Doro exchanged glances. Doro asked the woman, "Did Mrs. Volsanger leave a forwarding address?"

The landlady shook her head. "No, she didn't, and it's a shame too, because I wanted to send her a Christmas card. Such a charming person, so lovely, such a pleasant personality." And she closed the door.

"That," Allyn said disgustedly as they turned back to the car, "is just fine!"

"Especially the deaf part," Doro said. "That I like. Lee, I'll take it all back—all my doubts about your having a lead. The driver of the truck that figured in the Dawson getaway was a deaf man and wore a hearing aid. And I can't stretch coincidence to include the possibility of having two deaf people mixed up in the same murder case."

She got into the car, and when he'd joined her, he said, "Now play that over again, will you? The implication got by me, I'm afraid."

"Why, you dope, your Renard-Volsanger woman was the deaf 'man' who piloted the getaway truck!"

"Huh-uh."

"What do you mean?"

"Just—" he looked at her helplessly—"just huh-uh." He could not very well explain that Captain Zero had manhandled a certain deaf man on the night before, and there was not the slightest possibility that the blue serge suit could have contained the lush curves of Maria Renard.

"What's the matter with you this morning, Mr. Allyn?" she demanded hotly.

"Now don't start that Mr. Allyn business. I just said I didn't think Maria Renard was driving the truck. I don't think she's got a drivers' license."

"Nuts!" She jabbed indignantly at the starter button, would

have thrown the transmission into low if Allyn hadn't checked her, nodding to indicate the car that had pulled up in front of them.

THE MAN who got out looked neither to right nor left but hurried up the approach walk of the lodging house which they had just left. He was a well-dressed man, blond, his round boyish face incongruous with his stocky, mature figure.

"That's Henshaw," Allyn told the girl. "If he gets in we've been given the run-around."

"Maybe he lives there."

"He doesn't. He's from Indianapolis. If he doesn't get in, we'd better follow him. You'd better pull away from here right now."

"How are you going to follow him if you pull away from here?"

"Go around the block or something. He'll ask for Maria and the landlady will say, 'Oh my, you're the second party who has been after her in the last five minutes.' And then she'll point us out to him."

Doro accelerated away from the curb to make a right turn at the corner. When they'd completed the circuit of the block, Allyn pointed out Arthur Henshaw's shiny blue sedan rolling along the street a block ahead of them.

At the next corner Henshaw turned over to Keyes Avenue, one of the main east-west arteries of the city. Here the traffic was heavier and Doro decided they'd better tail the other more closely. She was jockeying for a position when Allyn said:

"He's got you spotted. Caught you in that side mirror when you came around that bus."

The girl didn't say anything but thrust out her chin determinedly and toed down on the gas pedal as Henshaw spurted ahead.

"Is there, or is there not, something highly peculiar about Mr. Arthur Henshaw?" Allyn asked triumphantly as the blue sedan widened the gap between them.

Doro didn't answer. She glanced into the rear vision mirror and then took off after Henshaw's car.

"Hey!" Allyn protested. "People get killed this way."

"You started it," she said. "You wanted to follow him."

"But right now I think I'd rather stop somewhere and have a nice strong cup of black coffee. I haven't had any breakfast."

Ahead of them was a traffic light, green now, changing to red as Henshaw neared the intersection. Doro smiled slightly and put on what she supposed would amount to a final burst of speed that could catch Henshaw. But Henshaw sailed right through the red light. So did Doro's Plymouth, though she had to throw the coupé into a screaming swerve to avoid a taxi that had started out into the intersection from the north. Almost at once they heard the wail of a police siren.

"Damn!" Doro said.

"Or, another way to put it, damn good," Lee Allyn said. "I've spent all the time in the hospital I want to for a while."

Doro had pulled over to the right-hand lane and was slowing down, possibly in the hope that the cop would give her the go-by in favor of Mr. Henshaw who was rapidly vanishing in the distance. But the cop pulled abreast and waved her to the curb.

"I guess I don't have to tell you what you did," the cycle officer said, grinning, as Doro cranked down the window.

"We were following that car ahead," she said, "and *he* went through."

The cop put his hand out for Doro's license. "Like mama used to say, 'Are you going to do everything you see the bad little boys do?'"

"But we're reporters," Allyn protested. "Didn't you see the press clip on the license plate?"

"That I did," the cop replied, busily writing in his summons book, "and I said to myself, 'Here is where Officer Murphy gets mention in the public press for being alert, efficient, and courteous.'"

"Murphy?" Doro crowed and clapped her hand. "My mother's name! And my father was a Kelly!"

"Sure and it's a couple of foin Irish names," the cop said mockingly, "and here's your ticket, Miss Kelly. See that you don't go through any more traffic lights unless they're a-wearin' o' the green!"

A FEW minutes after nine o'clock, Lee Allyn and Doro Kelly entered the *World* office. While Doro went off to powder her nose, Allyn tossed his hat onto his desk and sauntered over to the door of the teletype room from which Fritz Schoof and Editor Fairish had just emerged, Schoof caught Fairish's arm and pointed at Lee Allyn.

"It's a bird! It's a plane! It's Superman!"

Allyn flushed slightly.

"Yeah, you're supposed to be in the hospital," Fairish said, "How come?"

"Well, it's like this," Allyn said, "I just couldn't keep myself away from my work." Since Allyn, of necessity, spent as large a portion of his office hours as possible asleep with his feet on his desk, Fairish couldn't fail to catch the irony in the remark. Allyn hooked a thumb toward the teletype room, "Anything hot on the wires?"

Fritz Schoof chuckled. "A couple of honeys just came in. Our Senator Dunnwoody is out in the Rockies on some sort of water power survey, and he claims he lost his guide. It wouldn't occur to the Senator that possibly *he* might be the one who got lost. Not Dunnwoody. He's always right."

Fairish said, "I hope if that Federal power project for the Eastern Seaboard goes through that Dunnwoody is right that time. He's chairman of the committee, and I hope he kills the damned thing."

"What's this other honey?" Lee Allyn wanted to know. He took out cigarettes which he passed around.

"A matter of homing pigeons," Fairish told him. "Remember that stuffed-shirt Major Roscoe Brun who tried half a dozen times to get his name in the paper during the Dawson trial?"

Allyn nodded. " 'You-May-Quote-Me' Brun. Sure. He wrote a book once on murder trials. What's he got to do with homing pigeons?"

"When he got home last night—he lives in Indianapolis— he found his homing pigeons weren't. He raises the things, you know, claims to have learned a lot about them when he was in

Army Intelligence work. He immediately reported to the police that his pigeons had been stolen during his absence."

"What the hell would anybody want with them?" Schoof speculated. "Even with the price of fowl what it is. Anyway, Indianapolis is full of pigeons."

Somebody put a head out of the teletype room and said, "Hey, fellas," and ducked back.

Schoof, Fairish and Allyn went through the door. Jim Caster was in front of one of the teletype machines. Schoof and Fairish fell in on either side of him, leaving the tailback spot for Lee Allyn who was a good head shorter than any of the rest. Schoof swore. So did Fairish. Allyn took hold of Schoof's arm and tried to pull him aside.

"What is it? Come, on, give a little."

Schoof didn't yield his position. "Ivars," he said. "Burton Ivars, the Indianapolis banker. The boy that rumor has spotted for Secretary of the Treasury if there's a Cabinet."

"What'd he do, for cripesake?"

Fairish said, "Phi Gang!" and wheeled suddenly, his face florid, "We've got to spot a man up there."

"Me," Allyn said.

Fairish's eyes brushed past Lee Allyn and through the door of the room, "Kelly!" he shouted. "Hey, Kelly."

Allyn looked at the trim and graceful figure approaching the door. He said, "She doesn't look like a man to me."

FAIRISH WENT out to meet Doro, and Allyn followed. Fairish caught Doro by the shoulders. "You're going up to Indianapolis. Right now. They've found Burton Ivars' car—sans

Ivars—out near Carmel. Evidence of a struggle, and on the seat of the car a piece of paper with that Greek letter on it—phi."

Doro's eyes were wide and shiny with excitement. "Murder or snatch?"

"Don't know," Fairish panted. "You get the hell up there and stick with it, see?"

Allyn took a shallow breath. This could be it—the big job, the coup that Cavanaugh had predicted was coming. And Allyn had to get in on it. He had to because that was the only way to get Captain Zero in on it.

"Hey!" He caught Fairish by the arm, and Fairish looked around, down, and scowled. Allyn pointed at Doro who was racing across the city room toward her desk. "I'm going with her. Who eye-witnessed the murder of James Oliver yesterday? Was it Kelly? And who pinned Sam Dawson to the sidewalk? Was that Kelly, too?"

Fairish was shaking his head. "You're on the sick list. You're supposed to be in the hospital expecting a brain concussion. I'm not going to send you out on an assignment like this, have you drop dead, and then have your heirs suing the paper."

"Dammit, I haven't got any heirs at all!"

"Why don't you send Allyn up to cover the big pigeon snatch?" Fritz Schoof suggested facetiously, coming out of the teletype room.

Fairish snapped his fingers. "Say, that's an idea!"

"Cut it out," Allyn snapped helplessly.

"No, I'm serious. Remember that rib-tickler you did about the theft of that truck load of girdles last month, Allyn? Do something like that on Brun and his pigeons. That guy Brun sure burns me up, to coin a witticism. As long as you and Kelly can go up there on the same tank of gas, you get the dope on the homing pigeon homicide, or whatever it is, and we'll give Major Roscoe Brun some publicity he maybe won't want."

Doro Kelly was assigned to the big story while Lee Allyn literally got the bird. Well, if it wasn't the best way, it was one way. One way to get Captain Zero where he was needed.

Allyn sprinted the length of the room, snatched up his hat from the desk as he passed, and joined Doro Kelly in the corridor.

"I made it," he said, grinning triumphantly.

She took his arm. The warm smile on her lips reached up into her eyes where it really meant something.

"Lee, I'm glad," she said simply.

So he traveled most of the distance to Indianapolis in a rose-tinted cloud from which Doro managed to yank him when they were a few miles from the city.

"I was right about that mark, wasn't I?"

"Huh? How's that?" He sat up straight and blinked at her.

"Phi, or whatever it is." She drew an oval in the air and put a diagonal through it. "It's the trademark of the gang."

"U-m-m, maybe," he said.

"What do you mean, 'U-m-m, maybe'? Of course that's what it is. What else could it be?"

He looked at her and his smile was watery. He knew this was going to start an argument, and up to now everything had been just right between them. But he said it anyway.

"Red herring," he said; adding hastily, "Now don't blow up. A gang of professional crooks like that leaving a trademark at the scene of the crime—why, it's childish. It couldn't happen east of Hollywood."

"But it *is* happening," she insisted hotly. "A piece of paper with that sign on it *was* found on the seat of Barton Ivars' car.

"Then it is intended to confuse and distort the picture. Which, if you ask me, is plenty distorted right now."

CHAPTER 9
MASTER STROKE!

IT WAS nearly 4:00 P.M. when Lee Allyn arrived at the ancestral home of Roscoe Brun—*Major* Brun if you please. Situated on a large corner lot on North Delaware Street, the house was staunchly built of red brick with steeply pitched, slate-covered gables. There were coy, peeping balconies, a bracketed minaret complete with weather-cock, stained glass transoms, a walled garden at the back, and a carriage house with an ornate cupola.

The servant who admitted Allyn must have been nearly as old as the house. He accepted Allyn's press card impassively, and as he turned and crossed the gloomy hall to carry it to his master, his joints creaked. Brun, wearing a gray smoking jacket, received the reporter cordially in a towering library somewhere near the rear of the complex and aimless structure.

"Really, a most amazing thing!" he bellowed and left off pumping Allyn's hand. "But have a chair, my boy, have a chair.

You are here about—" the smudgy eyebrows lifted—"the pigeons, aren't you? Good!" The major's round red face shone like a polished apple in the glow from the coal-burning grate. He did not sit down but faced Allyn, his short, thick legs widely spread, his hands in the pockets of his jacket.

"They were stolen, of course," he said, "during my absence. I was in Pendleville, as you probably know, an interested observer at the Dawson trial, and upon my return I discovered that the house had been entered and all of my trained birds stolen."

"Trained birds?" Allyn put in. "I was under the impression that homing pigeons were born that way."

The major laughed. "Ah. Ah-ha! The popular notion. The homer is a variety of common pigeon in which the love of home and power of flight have been developed through generations of careful breeding, it is true. But the birds have to be trained to return to the loft, beginning with short distances at first.

"A mile the first time, then three miles a day or two later. Then twelve, twenty-five, fifty, seventy-five, ninety-six, one hundred and twenty-five, one hundred and fifty-five, and finally two hundred miles—those are the successive distances of flights made during the training period."

Brun's dark, blunt eyes were fixed on Allyn's face. "Didn't know that, did you?" he crowed loudly. "Most people don't. That's material for an article right there, isn't it? But let me show you the loft. I've some young birds up there. Lieges, you know. Not Antwerps. Most breeders in the United States go in for Antwerps."

And he kept right on talking as he led Lee Allyn out of the

library into a hallway that was almost dark, up two narrow flights of stairs into a garret beneath the peaked gable at the rear of the old house. The far end was partitioned off with wire mesh nailed to narrow wood uprights. There were wire cages along the side of the attic room, cages containing young pigeons.

"Pure Liege stock," Brun said proudly and then launched into a discourse which was intended to point out the superiority of the Liege variety over the Antwerp. Allyn attempted to maintain a polite interest, standing in the chilly garret, slightly nauseated by the smell of the place.

SLOW, DRAGGING footsteps climbed the stairs. The gray face of the ancient servant appeared in the doorway. Brun broke off in mid-sentence and frowned, two deep, black wrinkles forming a V between his eyebrows.

"What is it, Bartlet?"

"Mr. Nolan, sir."

The frown dissipated. "Ah! Reg Nolan, of course. Show him up, by all means!"

The servant hesitated a moment, then turned without a word and left them.

"Reg Nolan," Major Brun repeated the name for Allyn's benefit. "A brilliant attorney. He defended Dawson, you know."

Allyn was nodding. "I was at the trial, remember? In the press row."

The huge, tawny-haired attorney stepped into the loft, instinctively ducking his head as he passed under the lintel. And while the major was enthusiastically pumping Nolan's hand, Nolan's sullen eyes and dour mouth expressed distaste for the present surroundings.

"Good lord, Roscoe, you're not serving cocktails up here in this stinking loft, are you?"

Brun laughed and, turning to Allyn, said, "Reg doesn't share my enthusiasm for pigeons. By the way, have you met Mr. Nolan? Reg, this is young—uh, was the name Allyn?"

Allyn shook hands with Nolan who said, "A reporter, aren't you? I noticed you in court yesterday." He added with gruff malice, "Sleeping."

Allyn flushed. "Maybe I slept because I didn't have much doubt about the outcome." That created an uneasy silence in which the two older men both stared at him.

"Then you missed your calling, Allyn," Nolan said dryly. "Your guess was better than mine."

"Yes, well—" Brun coughed—"to change the subject from one crime to another, Allyn is here about the pigeons—my stolen birds, you know, Reg."

Nolan nodded. "I read about that. Who would want the damned things? What good are they to anybody besides you? If the thief turned them loose they wouldn't fly anywhere but back here."

"Breeding purposes, of course!" Brun bellowed. "The Liege is a comparatively rare strain, as I've been pointing out to Allyn. I've a tidy little sum tied up in those birds. A very tidy little sum."

Nolan had raised his head, rather carefully because of the rafters, and was staring over the major's head and into the far end of the loft.

"Roscoe, is that one of the family, or just a tramp looking for a handout?"

Brun and Allyn turned. A rather small, sleek pigeon had alighted on the ledge beyond one of the little arched openings cut through the gable wall. It now waddled through the arch, into the wire mesh cage, and began busily pecking at scattered grain.

Sam Dawson

"That's a Liege!" Brun said huskily. "It must be—it's *got* to be one of mine!" He hurried to the mesh partition, opened it, went to the small cage that contained the lone bird. As he opened the cage door he said excitedly, "It's Tilly! Tilly, I tell you! In the Chicago meet last year she flew home at the average velocity of twenty-four yards per second."

"Look at the man beam, will you," Nolan scoffed as Brun reached into the cage and captured the bird. "Tilly must have pecked the hand of the big, bad pigeon-burglar."

BRUN, HIS shiny face wreathed in smiles, brought the bird over to the mesh partition where the other two were standing.

"It's Tilly!" He couldn't get over it. "It really is. Notice—" His smile was suddenly replaced by a puzzled expression as he fingered the tail feathers. "What's this?" He turned the captive

88

bird over and revealed a small translucent cylinder—it looked like goose-quill to Allyn—attached to the tail of the pigeon.

"A message!"

"Probably a demand for ransom," Nolan suggested sourly. "You cough up or all of Tilly's brothers and sisters go into a pie. Some damn thing like that."

Brun had detached the cylinder. He released Tilly, came through the door of the partition, and opened the piece of goose-quill with his penknife to remove the tightly rolled strip of paper it contained. As he spread the strip to its full length his frown deepened.

"Good lord!" he said. *"Good lord!"* The paper trembled in his grasp as he extended it for the others to read:

> Major Brun:
>
> This is our first communication.
>
> You will inform Mrs. Burton Ivars that her husband is alive and well.
>
> Whether or not he remains in that desirable condition depends on how well subsequent instructions are followed. Any deviation on your part, or on the part of Mrs. Ivars, will result in the immediate death of Burton Ivars.
>
> We anticipate your telling the police and have not the slightest objection.
>
> Ø

As he read the note from its curt opening to its brazen challenge at the end, Lee Allyn became conscious of an inner trembling that was one part excitement and one part cold fury. Here again was the hand of a master strategist. In stealing Brun's pigeons the gang had provided itself with a means of communication that defied any tracing.

"The damned blackguards!" Brun exploded. Yet it had an impotent, wholly ineffectual sound. As though he'd brandished a pin.

CHAPTER 10
WOLF TRAP

DORO KELLY looked across the candle-lit table in the Club #7 at the slight, pale young man opposite her. She felt rather fond of Lee Allyn this evening without knowing exactly why. He had not been particularly attentive. He had not talked much. He had seemed tired and grave. She, in turn, found herself relaxing. They were good for each other, she decided.

She leaned across the intimate little table in order to make herself heard above the orchestra without shouting.

"A penny for your thoughts, boy."

He shook his head vigorously as though to clear it out. "On account of inflation the price is a nickel, but on account of you're such a nice girl I'll tell you for free. The thing that keeps going through my head is: 'We anticipate your telling the police and have not the slightest objection.'"

She knew that he referred to the closing line in the snatch-act message which Roscoe Brun had received via carrier pigeon. She had been with Lee Allyn when he had wired this latest development in the Burton Ivars kidnaping to the *World* office in Pendleville late that afternoon.

"It keeps bobbing up in my brain," he said, "and every time it does, I see red."

She nodded. "That is what might be called 'unmitigated gall,' to coin a cliché."

"So Brun tells the police, and all they can do is stick around that pigeon loft and wait for more birds to show. Not," he added, "that we're accomplishing a whole lot more by just waiting here for *our* pigeon."

Arthur Henshaw, Lee meant. They were here at Club #7 acting on a tip Doro had obtained from Mack Trimble of the *Indianapolis Record.* Mack knew Henshaw as any news reporter is apt to know a town's more prominent ne'er-do-wells. He had informed Doro that Henshaw could be seen almost any night in Club #7 with the newest item in his already extensive collection of feminine charmers.

Doro had told Mack that she'd gone to school with Henshaw, and while that wasn't one of her most original fibs it was certainly better than letting Mack know that Henshaw represented a lead to the Phi Gang.

Up to now Arthur Henshaw had failed to appear, and it was quite late. It was—she noticed Lee Allyn looking at his watch—11:40. She knew perfectly well what to expect from Lee, probably the very next time he opened his mouth. He'd suggest that they get back to their respective hotel rooms. He'd quote Gracie Allen on the virtues of early-to-bed.

Lee looked up from his watch, and Doro thought, Here it comes.

"You look tired tonight, honey," he said. Which was a different approach to exactly the same subject.

"*I* look tired?" She reminded herself not to glare at him. There was no sense in ruining an otherwise pleasant evening with a quarrel over who looked the more tired. After all, maybe she did. Maybe the smile she was working up for him was a tired smile.

"Do you realize, Lee, that although we've had several dates together I have never seen you after midnight?"

"Nobody else has." He looked somewhat startled by his own reply. He blinked rapidly and added, "That is, no other girl has, so what are you worried about?"

"Worried?" she echoed, amazed and angered by his presumptuousness. Kelly, she told herself, you ought to crown the little shrimp! She gripped the edge of the table as though that was what she was going to crown him with, and then forced herself to relax. They were not going to quarrel. Not tonight. Tomorrow, maybe, but tonight had been altogether too nice to spoil. She brought out the smile again.

"We really ought to be getting back to the hotel," she said sweetly.

SHE HAD every intention of doing just that. But then after he'd picked up the check and had stepped around the table to help her with her wrap, she happened to look toward the door into the foyer and there was Arthur Henshaw alone, looking as though he'd lost his last friend.

He seemed older than he had been that morning in Pendleville. He was puffy about the eyes and pouty about the mouth, and the way he wavered around getting down the steps into the dine-and-dancery suggested that he had made at least a couple of other stops before arriving at Club #7.

Doro shrugged away from the wrap that Lee Allyn held for her. She looked up, caught his eye, then nodded toward Henshaw.

"Our pigeon," she said triumphantly.

He didn't even glance toward Henshaw. Lee's small face mirrored nothing whatever. He said, "Yes, I know. Aren't you going to wear your wrap? These spring nights are chilly."

"I am not going." She made a flat statement of it, neither snapping at him nor freezing him with her glance. There was no reason whatever to make a scene. "I came here to talk with Arthur Henshaw. I do not intend to leave until I have talked with him."

He stared at her. Then his pale eyes shifted to Henshaw who had found a table and was now giving an order to a waitress.

"I don't think he knows anything worth learning, Doro," Lee said gravely.

"Don't be silly," she argued. "He'll have the address of his girl friend, Maria Renard, alias Mrs. Volsanger."

"I doubt it."

"You didn't doubt it an hour ago."

He kept staring at her, a completely helpless, almost hopeless expression on his face. He swallowed.

"Suppose I just pick you up and carry you out of here?"

She laughed. "I'd scream, the head-waiter would interfere,

you would have to put me down to fight the head-waiter, and you would spend the night in the hospital—"

"That wouldn't do."

"—*and* I would still go over to Arthur Henshaw's table, and even to his apartment, if I had to, to find out about Renard-Volsanger."

Lee appeared genuinely shocked. She was a little shocked herself.

"You wouldn't do that," he said.

The bridge heaved and buckled and the police car skidded to a stop.

"What?" she asked innocently.

"Go to that wolf's apartment."

"I don't see why not. I'm quite a big girl now and anyway I don't think any risk is too great if there's the slightest chance of getting a lead on that gang of kidnapers and murderers."

Lee patted away a yawn and his eyes crossed slightly trying to get a glimpse of the watch he wore on the inner side of his left wrist.

"All right," he said quietly and turned on his heel and left. Left the table, subsequently left the cashier's cage, left the hat-check concession, and left the building. Left her sitting there alone in the crowd. Nakedly alone.

Her eyes went on tour and met other eyes. One of a male pair winked at her. She lowered her eyelids, put the Kelly nose up into the air, got quickly out of her chair, and draped her coat over her arm. Then she picked her way around the dance floor, taking plenty of time, trying not to be too obviously on her way to Arthur Henshaw's table.

SHE PAUSED now, standing beside Henshaw, not quite looking at him, aware that he was not quite looking at her. Ahead of her were the three carpeted steps to the foyer. She had only to walk to them, up them, and out.

Her mind wavered between doing just that and making a play for Henshaw. She closed her eyes for an instant and saw faces. The faces of dead men—James Oliver, the two police, the McClaren girl—nameless strangers. There were God only knew how many dead faces.

She opened her eyes and smiled. Smiled down at Arthur Henshaw. Henshaw didn't smile. His round face looked puzzled.

"Hello," she said brightly and dropped into the chair opposite his, her coat across her lap. "You're lonely, aren't you?"

"No, I'm with three other people," he said thickly, pointing to the four martinis he'd ordered in anticipation of the liquor curfew. "Winken, Blinken, and Nod—they all gotta have a drink too."

AS SHE bowed mockingly as though to acknowledge introduction to Henshaw's imagined, invisible guests, she found herself suddenly thinking of Captain Zero—where was he and why hadn't he taken a hand against the Phi Gang?

But then he might have. If the plot was as far flung as Lee Allyn seemed to think it was, Captain Zero might even now be working on another angle of it. He undoubtedly was.

And if she kept on and on, digging ever deeper into it, eventually she might reach the point where *he* was and they might meet, the way they had once before. The thought stirred warmly within her, and she reached out a hand for one of Henshaw's martinis.

"I'm Nod," she said and giggled the way she presumed she would giggle if she'd had too many martinis. "You can tell because I'm always nodding."

"To me you're nodding, all right," he said unpleasantly. "That's a pun. Get it?"

She matched his pout with one of her own. "Artie, don't be like that. I could be something if you'd let me. I could be your once-in-a-while."

He frowned as though his memory was laboring, trying to place her face in his private gallery of experiences.

"How did you know my name?"

"Why, all the girls know you, Artie," she said with some more of that giggling. "You are to the girls of Indianapolis what the Rose Bowl is to a big Nine football team. Or is it the big Ten again?"

She thought that last was pretty good, but it was a long time registering with Arthur Henshaw. He thought.

"I am?" he said finally. He started to shake his head and when he did that his loose mouth wabbled. When he stopped shaking his head his eyes came into focus slowly. "Not all the girls. There's one—she stood me up tonight."

He took Winken's and Blinken's martinis hand-running. Nod sipped a little of hers and poured the rest of it into the nice thick carpet close to the wall where she hoped it would not be noticed. She wanted Henshaw to be sufficiently liquored to give whatever it was he had to give, but she didn't want him to pass out cold.

Henshaw put the second glass down and waved at the waitress who immediately came to his table.

"Your check, Mr. Henshaw?" she asked.

"Check, hell. I want another drink."

The waitress smiled and shook her head. "You're just five minutes too late, Mr. Henshaw."

Henshaw scowled. "A helluva law." His eyes scouted across the table. "Where's my other martini?" he asked Doro.

"Nod drank it," she said.

He grunted. "And you're nodding to me. Get it?"

"I got it the first time, and it was awfully funny." Doro was not at all affronted. Nothing he could have said would have fazed her because he impressed her as belonging to a biological order somewhat below that of a yeast cell.

She asked if he'd like to dance with her.

"No, I wouldn't," he told her bluntly. But his eyes were beginning to examine her with a little more interest.

"Then tell Nod about the girl who stood you up," Doro urged. "I'm very understanding. I'm the understandingest girl you ever met."

He put his forearms on the table and leaned toward her. "She's a most beautiful creature God ever made. 'Long side her you're just—" he waved a soft white hand.

"I'm just nodding."

But he was looking at her with interest. A shiny-eyed, frightening interest.

"I did'n mean that, baby."

She kept smiling. Her lips ached with smiling. He caught hold of her hand and pressed it hard. His palm was soft and unpleasantly moist.

"Let's get outta here, huh? What say?"

Her heart stopped, then bounded madly. She took a breath that wouldn't go down deep enough to satisfy the pounding of her heart, and she closed her eyes and saw dead faces.

"All right, big boy." Smiling at him. "Know of someplace, quiet?"

It was then 12:15. They went out together, and there was

perhaps five minutes' delay before the club employee drove Arthur Henshaw's big blue sedan up in front of the door. Henshaw helped Doro in. He went around, settled himself under the wheel.

"We're off, baby." And he was not just saying that. Acceleration rammed her back into the soft cushions. She wanted to cover her face with her hands. It was the wildest eight blocks she had ever ridden. It was the longest ride and at the same time the shortest, for presently she was standing on the sidewalk in front of a swank apartment building on Maple Boulevard with the precious seconds hurrying away from her while Arthur Henshaw locked his car.

She stared at him, his boy's face on a man's body, the boy's mind behind the face. She was contemptuous and she was afraid, and the one counterbalanced the other so that in this short interval when she could have run, she didn't.

AND THEN it was too late. His hand was clutching her arm, and it was stronger than she had supposed a soft white hand could be. He was guiding her up the approach walk, into the hushed foyer and toward the front of the automatic elevator.

The elevator was small. She was thinking that when the door slid shut she wouldn't be able to breathe. She wouldn't be able to scream. And then as Henshaw fumbled along the row of control buttons, somebody came through the front door of the building and called, "Hold it, please."

The man was a doctor, Doro judged from the satchel he carried, a pleasant appearing man of about fifty. He said it was a lovely evening, and they agreed that it was.

"Fourth for you, isn't it, Doctor?" Henshaw asked after he'd pressed the button numbered 3 for himself.

The door closed, and Doro could breathe, for she was not yet alone with him. There were still precious fleeting seconds. Then the door opened, and his soft white hand was steering her out into the corridor. Her backward glance touched the face of the kindly doctor, but he was staring in a preoccupied manner at the floor of the elevator.

The fleeting seconds while Henshaw had trouble fitting his key into the lock of his door, and she thought that when he got it open she could give him a shove and then run. Run where? She glanced about, thinking that there must be a stairway some-place, and then it was too late. His white hand was on her upper arm, his fingers in her armpit.

"A nice quiet place, that whatchu said, baby?"

That was what she had said, and this was it. Quiet, at least—not nice. Too many low, soft couches, all broad and backless. Too much modern art upon the walls. She shivered as he helped her off with her coat, and that was a mistake.

"Cold, baby?"

"A—a little," she stammered and hastily handed him her hat. That would keep his hands busy for a while. His eyes, however, were on the loose. They were all over her at once. They approved.

"Baby, you're cute."

"Thank you, sir," she said and forced a giggle. "I've been in some of the better address books." She thought she'd better get onto the subject of address books right away, because that was what she was after—a look at his.

100

He was moving away from her now, her coat and hat in his arms. At the door leading into the next room he paused, looked back at her out of the corners of his eyes. He seemed puzzled, or possibly only confused by drink.

"I've seen you somewhere," he said.

"Why, Artie," she said, "how perfectly silly. Of course you have."

He nodded stupidly. "I thought so. I thought I'd seen you somewhere." He went out of the room, half closed the door, called to her from behind it. "Fix us a coupla drinks, huh, baby? Be with you inna jiff."

She moved over to the mahogany liquor cabinet from which she took a couple of old fashioned glasses into which she poured straight whiskey. It would give her something to throw in his face if she had to. It was not a reassuring thought—that she'd probably have to—and her hand trembled, slopping some of the liquor. As she put the decanter down, there was a satiny whisper of sound from the door through which he had entered. She turned, her mind numb with apprehension.

HE HAD removed his suit coat, had replaced it with—she might have known—a black satin dressing gown. It didn't go with his round boyish face. It didn't go with that unworldly, faintly puzzled expression he had.

"Where was it I saw you, baby?"

"Why, Artie," she said and batted her eyelashes at him as she sidled to the nearest couch and sat down on the edge of it. "Artie, how could you forget!" She took a little sip of the liquor. She needed it for that numbness in her mind. "And you said you'd never, never forget. You promised. And you put my name and 'phone number down in that little address book, remember?"

She pat the glass down on the cocktail table. He was coming toward her, and she just might need both hands.

"Nope." His mouth squashed out over the word and made it definite. "Notchu. Some I could maybe forget, but notchu. You're too damn' cute. You got too mucha what it takes to make memories."

"You did, you did!" She pounded on her knees with clenched fists and made a face which she hoped he would find repugnant "You wrote my name and address in your little book. I'll bet you. I'll bet you anything you want."

"Anything?"

"Yes. You get the book and I'll show you!"

A sly look came over his face. He turned, went across the room where he opened the top drawer of a knee-hole desk. He took out a slim, limp volume in blue leather with gold stamping, came to the couch and dropped down beside her. His nearness sickened her.

"Kelly, huh?" he mused. "An Irisher, huh?" Chuckling, he thumbed an index tab, flipped to the Ks. He raised his eyes and triumphed peeped out of them. "Nope. You're not there. Whatcha think of that, baby?"

"I am so! You cheated!" She snatched the book from his soft hands, twisted around on the couch so that she faced him and the address book didn't. She flipped to the V's for *Volsanger*. Except for a lady designated only by the name *Vivian* those pages were blank. She tried the R's. Here were many names. Her eyes sought feverishly for *Renard.* She turned the page. More Rs, but no *Renard.*

Cold disappointment rushed over her like a draft from an open window. She glanced up, saw his soft round face over the edge of the book, and the sly look he had. He took the book out of her unresisting hands, would have tossed it aside except that he noticed where she had opened it. The sly look was gone, displaced by confusion again.

Doro stood up carefully as though she were balancing a case of nitro on her head. She started to back away toward the door, though there was scant hope that she could reach it and get it open fast enough.

He said, "I thoughtchu said your name was Kelly. How come you looked under R. How come you did, if it's Kelly?" He stood up, and she tried holding him off with her eyes. If she backed any farther she'd make her intention clear and he would lunge at her. He seemed about to lunge right now, his body swaying forward slightly.

"It—it is," she stammered. "Doro Kelly, care of the Pendleville *World.*"

That did something to him. His eyes narrowed and his face became pale, slightly greenish. He made a sound like laughter.

"I think you think you're puttin' somethin' over on me," he said slowly.

And then he rushed at her. She fell back against the door, the back of her hand against her mouth to stifle the scream that rose in her throat.

CHAPTER 11
THE GREEN-EYED GODDESS

S HE DID not scream, and he did not reach her. It was as if a wall of glass stood between them. Or it was an invisible battering ram against which Henshaw blindly ran? It crumpled him. She heard the impact, saw Henshaw's distorted face, heard the *woosh* of air exploding from his lungs. Then he was backing very rapidly, doubled over, until his digging heels could no longer keep pace with his shifting center of gravity. Then he was sitting down on the floor and he was being awfully sick at his stomach.

Doro Kelly stood there, against the door, looking everywhere except at Arthur Henshaw, and her heart was doing crazy little nip-ups. And her mind sang, Captain Zero! He's here. *Somewhere.* Here in this room!

"Aren't you?" she whispered finally. "Captain Zero, isn't it?"

"Yes, angel."

Her searching gaze had gone far afield for he was directly in front of her. She felt his unseen hands close upon her shoulders, felt the warmth of them penetrating to her flesh.

"You're a good brave girl," his quiet, gentle voice was saying. *"Get the other address book out of the desk drawer. Couldn't you have guessed he wouldn't have played fair?"*

"Yes." Warm color rushed into her cheeks. "But then you don't understand. It wasn't *my* address—"

His soft laugh interrupted her. *"Of course not. Maria Renard's address. I understand. I was looking over your shoulder when you were going through the blue address book, contrary to all rules of etiquette. So if you'll try and find Renard's address in the red address book, right away, please."*

His hand fell away from her shoulders, and she moved to the knee-hole desk, opened the drawer from which she had seen Henshaw take the blue address book. There was another similar book with a red binding and an appearance of newness about it. Fingers trembling with excitement, she got it open to the Rs.

"Yes," she said. "It's here, Arlington Avenue, the Winston Apartments."

"Good." Zero's voice came from a spot somewhat above where Arthur Henshaw was sitting on the floor. *"Get your coat and hat, angel, out of the next room. And his car keys—he doesn't seem to have them in his trousers pockets. Then go down to his car and wait for me. What is of necessity about to happen to Mr. Henshaw here may not be too pleasant to witness."*

"Don't—" Henshaw began faintly, but groaned and stopped.

Doro flew into the bedroom for her hat, coat, and purse. She found the keys to Henshaw's car on the top of a chest of drawers, ran back into the living room, and to the door.

"Be with you in a little while, angel," Zero's voice promised her. *"Depending on how long its takes Henshaw to loosen up."*

She left without a backward glance for she could not see Zero and she certainly didn't want to see Henshaw ever again.

As soon as the door had closed behind the girl, Zero turned his attention to the man on the floor. He put out an invisible foot and prodded Henshaw with it.

"Get up."

Henshaw didn't get up. He scooted back a little way on the seat of his pants and screwed his eyes up tight.

Zero said mockingly, *"You're too old a boy to navigate like that. Get up on you hind legs, Henshaw."*

"You—you'll knock me down," Henshaw whimpered. "And I'm sick. I'm too sick to take anything like that."

"I'm not going to touch you," Zero said, *"if you'll talk. If you don't, I'll only touch you once. Because that's all it will take, and I'm getting awfully damned tired of seeing you around."*

HENSHAW GOT up warily and staggered to a couch. He flopped on it, groaning. "Just a second," he panted, "I'll talk. I'll tell you what you want to know." He got out his hankerchief, blew his nose violently. "Now," he said. "Now, I'll talk."

"Take it away," Zero said dryly.

"Well, I—I was in Canal Street in Pendleville the night the McClaren girl was murdered. And they had the right guy—Sam Dawson, I saw him come out of the alley, and he was wiping blood off his hands."

Henshaw rolled his eyes, looking for Zero. "Well, is that what you wanted to know?"

"No," Zero said. *"It's an interesting little sidelight on your character, Mr. Henshaw, but it is no longer essential information. If you'd come out with that in court it might have accomplished something. It might have even saved a life. Not that you give a good damn about anybody's life except your own."*

Henshaw rocked forward on the couch and took his face in his hands. A boy's face, blubbering.

"Stop that," Zero said disgustedly. He stepped over to

Henshaw and slapped the man's hands down. *"Why did you go to the Dawson trial?"*

"Bub—because I knew he did it. I wanted to see justice done."

"Oh, sure!" Acidly. *"So you sat there all through it with your mouth shut and watched justice done! Try again. Didn't you go because Maria Renard was there? You were following her, weren't you?"*

Henshaw laced his fingers over his tummy. "I—I think I'm going to be sick again."

"Answer me, and you can go be as sick as you want to. Maybe I'll go out and be sick too. You're enough to nauseate anybody."

"That—that's right," Henshaw admitted. "I followed Maria to Pendleville. When she went to the trial, I did too. She was up in the balcony, and she wouldn't give me a tumble. While the judge was charging the jury, I went over to where she was, and she made like she'd never seen me."

So that was what had ailed James Oliver in the jury box. He'd seen Henshaw approaching Maria. Call it jealousy on Oliver's part, or perhaps he felt he'd been played for a sucker—that there was another man in Maria's life. Then Maria had given Henshaw the brush-off, had waived a handkerchief or something at Oliver to assure him that everything was all right.

"Where was Maria when you left the gallery?" Zero asked.

Henshaw shook his head. "I don't know. She'd slipped out somehow in the crowd. Maybe to meet some other guy, I don't know. Because there was another guy in Pendleville. I did some detective work—describing her to a lot of barkeeps in the night spots—and she'd been around. She was using the name of Volsanger, I found out, but by the time I learned where she'd been staying, she'd left town."

Zero went over to the door. *"Stay away from her, Henshaw. There was another guy in Pendleville, just as you surmised. But do you know where he is now?"*

The man on the couch shook his head.

"In a casket," Zero said. *"They're burying him tomorrow."*

Henshaw shuddered.

"And do you know what happened to the other guy's wife because she was interested enough in the woman her husband was playing around with to find out it was Maria?"

"No. And for God's sake leave me alone!"

"They cornered her in a closet and pumped eight slugs into her." Zero opened the door. *"And I do hope you'll get a good night's rest, Mr. Henshaw."*

ZERO, WHO had come up to the third floor in the elevator along with Henshaw, Doro, and the doctor who lived on the floor above, now went quietly along the corridor until he found the stairway. He went down, left the building by a side entrance, walked out to the street where he found Doro Kelly pacing back and forth on the sidewalk beside Arthur Henshaw's blue sedan.

Zero touched her arm. She wheeled and uttered a slight, startled sound.

"I'm sorry," he said quietly. *"I always have a little trouble making my presence known without scaring the wits out of people. You have Henshaw's keys?"*

"Yes." She glanced toward the car. "But we're not—"

He laughed. *"Why not? Henshaw isn't going to make any trou-*

ble. After all, he enticed you into his apartment, didn't he, and the law is inclined to frown on such things. He'd have rather a hard job convincing the court that you were well chaperoned all the while."

"All the while?" she asked timidly.

"Yes. I've been with you all evening. Earlier, with you and Lee Allyn, of course," he added hastily. *"Now will you please get in and drive me to Arlington Avenue. I'm sorry to be so helpless, but traffic police are usually disturbed when they see a driverless car weaving in and out of traffic."*

She got into the car, in under the wheel. She fumbled the key into the ignition switch, and had some trouble finding the starter.

"Nervous?" he asked from the cushions beside her.

"Yes!" she said sharply. "Wouldn't you be?"

"I don't know," he said laughing. *"I've never taken an invisible lady for a ride. Only, of course, because I don't know any invisible ladies."*

She got the car started, let it roll out from the curb and into the wide boulevard.

"Arlington is east, I think," he said.

"You think? Don't you know? Aren't you familiar with Indianapolis?"

Danger, his mind rang like a tocsin. Doro, he knew, was not merely curious, she was also clever. He would have to be eternally on his guard against her efforts to penetrate the mystery of his identity.

"Not too familiar," he admitted. *"There are so many cities and there's only one of me."*

"How do you travel usually?" she persisted as she swung the car in a wide loop turn to get it heading east.

"With the wind," he said whimsically.

"Don't," she said flatly, and he noticed, in the light from the instruments that her chin trembled a little. "Don't kid a girl like that, will you?"

"Well then, I travel by train or bus. Seldom by plane because of the extra weight. It doesn't cost anything, but it's not relaxing. Too many people try to sit on me."

She drove on steadily and in silence. The clock on the dash indicated 1:10. When they had traveled perhaps a mile farther, Doro braked and swerved to angle in toward the curb.

"What's wrong?" he wanted to know.

"Arlington. We just passed it. Didn't you see the sign?"

"No." He paused. He couldn't tell her that his distance vision was poor. She knew just how near-sighted Lee Allyn was. *"I'm afraid I'm a bit absent-minded."*

She waited for a couple of cars to breeze by before she swung the blue sedan around and headed back.

"Are you always like this?"

It was one of the questions he had been expecting and had wondered how to answer. He stalled.

"Absent-minded, you mean?"

Her laugh was strained. "Absent period. Invisible."

AND HE still didn't have the answer. If he told her the truth—that he was invisible only from midnight to dawn—she'd be apt to connect this with Lee Allyn's stubborn refusal to be seen after midnight. He'd slipped up once on that subject already.

110

"I'm always like this," he lied finally.

"Then—then it isn't true, what they say—that you're just a normal man who has mastered a clever illusion."

"No," he said sadly. *"That isn't true except in part: I'm just an ordinary man—"*

Her wild laughter, bordering on hysteria, interrupted him. He said, *"Now wait a second, angel."*

"I can't help it!"

"Cut that out. I've got to have your help tonight. We can't put our little selves ahead of the public welfare. This Phi Gang is bigger than you or me."

"But I've *got* to know! Try and put yourself in my place. I'm driving along through the dark in a stolen car toward God knows where. I'm alone. Yet I'm not alone. I've got a hitch-hiker who's nothing but a voice. It—it's all too damned near the brink of insanity!"

He put his arm about her shoulders. She became quiet, and some of the nervous tension went out of her.

"Now," he said gently. *"I am a normal, ordinary man."* It was a thought he clung to obstinately. *"But I offered myself as the subject for certain scientific experimentation. Think of me as a victim, if you wish, of radioactive particles gone wildly off the beam. There are things in the world which you cannot see but which you accept as reality. The air, for instance. Can't you accept me in the same way?"*

"Can try," she said bravely. "It's like being blind. Isn't it?" That startled him. Lee Allyn had been blind, and Doro knew it. "If I were blind," she went on, "the world would be full of Captain Zeros."

"You're not driving with your eyes shut, are you, just to see what it's like to be blind?" he asked with an uneasy laugh. *"Because we just passed the Winston. Now, keep on going for a couple of blocks and then turn back. We've got to get our plans straight. I feel reasonably sure Maria Renard is a member of the Phi Gang, and if she is I can't just barge in there. They've all been alerted to expect me, and they're too handy with a paint spray."*

He told her briefly what had happened on the previous night. He went on.

"I want you to go to Maria Renard's apartment, knock at the door until you get the lady to open it. While you're explaining that you've got the wrong address or something, I can slip in without alarming. Got that, angel?"

"Roger," she said as she turned the car about in the middle of an intersection and headed back toward the Winston Apartments.

They stepped into the vestibule of the four-story walk-up apartment building, and the old telegram gag looked as promising as any for getting past the electric lock on the main entrance. Doro pressed the button above a mailbox designated as that of one Albert Dark who lived on the top floor. A sleepy feminine voice finally came from the speaking tube, and it was Zero who responded. He had, he said, a telegram to deliver to Mr. Clark. The electric lock buzzed, Doro pushed the door open, and then waited bewilderedly for the invisible Zero to enter.

"Not like that," his whisper cautioned. *"Just ignore me when it comes to doors. I'll squeak through."*

MARIA RENARD'S apartment was C-3. When Doro got

to the top of the third flight of stairs, she faltered. Her face had a pale, drawn look, and her chin was trembling. Zero cupped her elbow in his palm and urged her gently forward. He didn't dare risk even a whisper of reassurance. This was Doro's part of the job, and she had to carry it through.

She faced the door. She raised her fist, and Zero saw her knuckles whiten. Her knock was sharp, determined, and almost immediately the door was opened wide enough to disclose a narrow face. A man. Somebody with center parted hair that might have been applied with two strokes from a brush dipped in black enamel. Cold, expressionless gray eyes passed quickly over Doro's trim figure. There was a gleam of white, white teeth.

"Yes?"

"Mr. Clark?" Doro asked faintly.

The man didn't say anything for a moment. He kept looking at her. Then his sleek head wagged from side to side.

"You've got the wrong party." He still hadn't opened the door wide enough for Zero to get through, and Doro must have realized this. Her left hand went out in a tremulous gesture.

"But—but that's Mrs. Clark sitting there." She must have been able to see someone beyond the man whom Zero could not from his position.

The man lifted an eyebrow sardonically. "Mrs. Clark? It is?" He opened the door wider and stood back a pace.

Beyond a small vestibule, Maria Renard sat in a chair in the living room. She raised her eyes from the magazine on her lap— her wonderful jade green eyes.

Doro Kelly put a hand up to her throat. "Oh," she said as

113

though in surprise. "Oh, I'm terribly sorry. I—I must have the wrong address. But just from as much of you as I could see, I thought it was Mrs. Clark. Forgive me, won't you?"

She was backing away, and the man with the black enameled hair still stood in the open door and watched her.

"Yes, of course," he said finally. "We all make mistakes."

He closed the door, and Doro turned and fled to the stairs.

Zero was in. He was immediately behind the man when the latter closed the door. He sidled away as the man turned and stepped back into the living room. Zero remained in the vestibule. The floor beneath him was waxed asphalt tile. The floor of the living room was covered from wall to wall with thick, resilient carpet in a deep shade of rose. Had it been a two-inch snowfall it couldn't have offered a better medium for recording Zero's footprints.

So he kept to the vestibule, watched the man cross to a large glass-topped coffee table from which he took a cigar that had rested on the rim of an ash tray. Maria Renard turned a page of her magazine. A slight frown strayed across her perfect brow.

"That girl, Gil," she said. "I've seen her somewhere before. I'm sure I have."

"Have you?" He unconcernedly lighted his cigar. "What was wrong with her?"

"Wrong?"

"She looked scared to me," he said. "Certainly nervous."

Maria didn't say anything but sat there, her lovely head ripped to one side as though listening. Finally, she got up and went into the end of the room where Zero could not see her. He

114

moved forward carefully to the very edge of the carpet, took hold of the door frame with invisible fingers, and leaned into the room without moving his feet. Maria Renard was standing at a window looking down onto the street.

The man dropped into a chair. There was a certain grace about his movements suggesting that he might have been a dancing master. A Latin of some sort, judging by his dark, oily skin.

He said, "But to get back to the subject, if you're Number Three, you're pretty close to the top man. You ought to know what the next move is."

"I don't," Maria said with a touch of exasperation. "No one knows. He keeps everything under that black hat of his. I do what I'm told to do, and I advise you to do the same."

The man drew thoughtfully on his cigar, blew a thin wisp of smoke ceilingward.

"Who's Number Two, do you know?"

"There isn't any Number Two." Maria laughed unpleasantly. "He asked too many questions, so now there isn't any."

Gil cocked an eyebrow. "Like that, huh?"

Maria glanced back at him over a slightly elevated shoulder. The smile didn't quite touch her narrow, jade green eyes.

"Like that. Just do as you're told and don't ask questions. Don't even think any more than you can help. The cops can't touch you. No one in our organization actually knows who you are except Black Hat himself. Play square with him, and you'll do all right for yourself. Play it any other way, and you'll either find yourself in the hands of the law or on the end of a tag in the city morgue."

The woman turned back to the window. Gil stared at her,

at the creamy flesh revealed in a long V by the low-cut black evening dress.

"Would you kill me, Maria," he asked evenly, "if Number One ordered you to?"

She shrugged, still looking out of the window, "it wouldn't come that way. It wouldn't be anybody you knew. Some stranger. You'd be walking down a crowded street in New York, and suddenly you'd drop with a knife in your back. Or it would be in Chicago, in a crowded bar, and somebody would drop cyanide into your drink. Or right here on a dance floor. Anywhere and anybody. These are so many of us."

MARIA BROKE off suddenly. Zero, leaning into the room from the vestibule, saw the woman's hand clutch at the rose drapery.

"Gil, that girl—"

The man flicked at a bit of cigar ash on his dress trousers. "What about her?"

"She's sitting in a car across the street."

"Probably trying to figure out where the Clarks live."

"They live upstairs," Maria told him. "I don't think she wanted the Clarks. She'd have gone up to the next floor if she'd really thought she'd made a mistake. She's just sitting in that car, waiting."

"You've got the jitters."

"Maybe. But I think I've seen her before. In Pendleville."

"Suppose you have?"

"If it's the same girl, then she's a reporter. And I *know* whose car that is."

Gil stared at Maria's back. "What do you want me to do?"

Maria turned from the window. "Go down and get her."

He frowned.

"Right away, Gil. We can't take chances."

The man stood up uncertainly. "She won't like it. She'll raise a fuss."

The green eyes looked him coldly up and down. "And if she does? You'll know what to do, won't you? Or must I draw you a blueprint?"

The man's lips twisted into a watery smile. "I'll know. I'll run your little errand for you. I'm on my way right now."

He only thought he was on his way. His soft gray hat was lying on the table to the left of the door which meant that he had to cross the mouth of the vestibule to reach it. Inexplicably he tripped, sprawled full length beside the table.

"Clumsy!" Maria called him and stamped her foot.

He was anything but that, and he knew it. Something had tripped him. With the supple grace of a tumbler, Gil bounded to his feet, stared down at the floor. There was nothing there, not so much as a ripple in the carpet. A puzzled expression on his face, he entered the vestibule.

Had he run into coiled steel springs that were instantly released he could not have been ejected more quickly and forcibly from the vestibule. He back-stepped the width of the room where he was stopped by the mantelpiece of a dummy fireplace.

"Gil, *he's* in here!" Maria, eyes glinting with alarm, stared toward the man in front of the fireplace.

Gil's dark eyes were fixed on the vestibule. His face had a

yellowish pallor, a tautness. From immobility that was almost statuesque he came suddenly to life, his movements blending into a blur of motion that from somewhere produced and then threw a slim-bladed knife. To Zero, standing in the vestibule, it was like a brief, blinding ray of light from a small mirror that has momentarily caught the rays of the sun. He dropped to one knee, heard the *thuck* as the knife nailed the panel of the door behind him, sprang from a crouch to land ten feet from where Maria and the man were standing.

"Easy, baby," Gil said out of the corner of his mouth. "He's not so tough. He can't carry any weapons, don't forget. Don't let him slip out of here."

GIL MOVED again from that position of immobile tautness. There was a second knife—this from the sleeve of his dinner jacket—and he struck out with it, slashing the air, as he sprang toward the spot where footprints on the carpet clearly indicated the presence of Captain Zero.

But then the footprints were gone. Gil recovered quickly from the spent force of the knife thrust. His gaze flung about the carpeted floor.

"Where the hell is he?"

Out of seemingly thin air and somewhat above their heads the soft voice of Captain Zero spoke to them.

"The people who have asked that question, laid end-to-end, would keep an undertaker busy for months."

"Gil, he's standing on the coffee table!" Maria cried.

It was a very original idea. Considering that the top of the coffee table was made of glass which certainly would have shattered beneath Zero's weight, it was perhaps too original. But Gil was willing to buy it.

He sprang and slashed, again at the air, and Zero stepped nimbly down from the spindly straight chair on which he had been standing, picked up the chair which was a good deal heavier than it looked—and swung it in a wide arc.

The chair struck Gil's knife wrist. There was a snapping sound as of wood breaking, though it was not necessarily a chair rung that had broken. The knife went spinning off somewhere. The chair was poised for an instant, and then it sailed across the room to catch Maria's flat tummy in the fork of its legs.

Maria may have assumed that Zero was on the other end of the chair, for she screamed to Gil for help. Gil started toward her, ran squarely into Captain Zero, whose unseen hands clamped on Gil's lean throat.

They rocked backward together, Gil and Zero, fell alongside the coffee table, Zero on top, fingers still on the other's neck. Zero knew suddenly that he was going to have to kill the shiv artist, that there was no other way except retreat; that retreat was unthinkable for, unless he checked it here, the news that Doro Kelly was associated with Captain Zero would quickly spread along the Phi Gang grapevine.

That was the general idea—to kill Gil. But then Gil was a combination bucking bronco and eel, and his left arm was free, his fist pouring blow after blow into the small of Zero's back which was very small indeed and not at all well padded. Had it not been for Maria's attempt to assist Gil, Gil might have got the best of it after all.

But as Zero began to wonder how long he would be able to hang onto Gil, he saw, out of the tail of his eye and in the reflecting surface of the coffee table top, the beautiful and evil face of Maria Renard above him. And he saw the knife in her hand.

Zero kicked out wildly and rolled to the right without slackening his hold on the other man. Maria might have fallen over something, maybe somebody's leg, for there was an overabundance of legs. Or Zero might have kicked her at the very moment when she was off balance in her attempt to check the downward thrust of the knife in her hand.

Whatever it was, Maria was suddenly on top of them. More particularly, she was on top of Gil. Maria screamed. Gil—it was certainly Gil with his white dress shirt—flattened on top of Zero's face. Gil was still struggling but it was as though with some other opponent than Zero. With Death Itself, maybe, Gil was struggling.

ZERO SHOVED Gil off and rolled out from under. As he got to his feet he glimpsed Maria making tracks through a connecting door. He lurched after Maria, and she slammed a door in his face. He got the door open, started across her bedroom, and she slammed another door just beyond.

This one was locked—a bathroom door—and she'd bolted it on the other side. He tried his shoulder against it, which proved an impractical idea he'd got from the movies. He staggered across the bedroom for a boudoir chair, aware that, on the other side of the door, Maria was speaking in clipped, frantic syllables.

"Calling GHQ. Calling One. Three calling One. Calling—" And then a small but choice selection of unprintables as Maria, in a burst of temper, kicked something—hardly a bucket, but that was the sound effect. A metal waste basket, perhaps.

Zero came lunging back with the chair, rammed at the door with it. A leg splintered. He stood at the side of the door and swung the chair like an ax. This time a small panel on the door close to the lock gave way at the corner. He shoved the panel all the way out with his foot, got a hand through, twisted the bolt handle, got the door open, lurched into the room. And she wasn't there.

The window was open and tied to the radiator beneath it was a thin, tough-looking white rope.

Zero thrust his head out of the window, saw nothing but darkness below. He twisted around, his gaze jumping from stool to tub to lavatory—all perfectly ordinary pieces of plumbing incapable of concealing a radio station. He opened a door, and that was the linen closet so well supplied with shelves as to be incapable of concealing Maria.

He ran out of bathroom and bedroom. In the living room, Gil wasn't doing anything; he wouldn't be doing anything ever again. Zero went into the vestibule, out the front door, and ran down the three flights of stairs.

Across the street, the engine of Henshaw's car kicked over as the front door of the building fanned wide open. Zero ran toward it, half afraid that the girl at the wheel was not Doro but Maria Renard.

"You, angel?" he panted.

"When I saw the door open and no one come out, I knew it was you." And Doro started to laugh.

"Don't." He got the door of the car open, dropped to the cushions beside her. *"Did you see Maria? She's slipped out of the building—did you see her?"*

"No."

"Then she went up the alley. Try that. We've got to catch her, angel. It won't be healthy for you if we don't."

CHAPTER 12
ZERO-HUNT

I N HIS garage building headquarters on Market Street, the Man in the Black Hat stared across the dimly lighted room and through the one-way mirror at Maria Renard motionless in her chair, her body taut, her hands clenched on her purse.

"You are certain you were not followed?" his metallic voice snapped at her.

"Certain." Maria swallowed past the dryness in her throat. "I lost the blue sedan in Irvington. You know what the streets are like out there—a veritable maze. I didn't even head this direction until I was certain that I had given them the shake."

The Man in the Black Hat was thoughtfully silent.

"And you couldn't get a call through, either to me or to anyone in that sector?" he asked finally.

"No, I couldn't. The damned radio wouldn't work. Zero hit me with a chair, and I think that must have done it. Anyway, it was dead. As dead as—" she shivered slightly—"as Gil must be right now."

She had already told him how, in the struggle, she had fallen on Gil with the knife in her hand.

"You weren't—" the Man in the Black Hat paused—"in love with Thirty-four, were you?"

"With Gil?" Maria's lips curled scornfully. "Don't be absurd! But he's there in my apartment with a knife in his back, and I'm in a spot. You've got to move me. Send me to Chicago, New York, anywhere—only get me away from here."

"When you return to your apartment," Black Hat said, "and you *will* return, there will be no body. I have already given orders for its removal. You have nothing to fear from the police. And you will return because you constitute valuable bait at the present moment. Bait with which we shall certainly trap this Captain Zero.

"Tomorrow you will be given a new assignment, an extremely important one. On your way back to your apartment, you will turn your radio in for a new one. I shall keep in touch with you."

Maria opened her purse, took out a slim cigarette case. The flame of her lighter reflected the nervousness in her fingers. When she had her cigarette going, she asked:

"What about the girl—the reporter?"

"I—uh, don't quite know," the Man in the Black Hat said slowly.

"It was she who tried to follow me," Maria insisted. "And in Arthur Henshaw's car. She's in some way associated with Captain Zero, I know damned well she is. And what was she doing with Henshaw's car?"

The Man in the Black Hat laughed harshly. "I'm sure I haven't the slightest idea. Strangely, Number Three, I am much more concerned with the present state of your nerves than I am with any small-town reporter who may be somewhat suspicious of you. I have never seen you nervous before, and I don't like it. I've come to depend on you, perhaps too much."

Ash trembled from Maria's cigarette. "I'm not nervous, Hat. Call it by its real name. Call it fear. How can you fight back against something you cannot see?"

The Man in the Black Hat stood up, crossed the dimly lighted room to the mirror door. His black gloved hand poised for a moment above the doorknob, then dropped to it, twisted it, pulled the door open.

Maria jerked out of her chair and to her feet. She stood with lips apart, her jade green eyes staring at the bulky figure that approached. His black gloved hand lifted, brushed up the brim of the pork-pie hat so that the light fell across his face.

"You!" she gasped. She took a single backward step, then stood rooted to the spot. The Man in the Black Hat was directly in front of her.

"Disappointed, Maria?"

"No!" she stammered. "Surprised. Not disappointed."

He put a powerful arm about her slim waist and drew her to him. "This," he said softly, "is something I have wanted to do for a long time. You've been my good right arm, Maria, for over a year now, but you are rapidly becoming much more than that. I didn't want it that way. I didn't want to fall in love with you, but then I have. I thought it might help you to know that you have nothing to fear. I couldn't let anything happen to you, understand?"

The woman raised her head. Her eyes were shining. "Kiss me," she whispered. "And hold me tight for a moment. I'll be all right."

He kissed her. And then, "Together, Maria, we can carve out an empire. Nothing can stop us. Not even a phony called Captain Zero."

"No, nothing."

He kissed her again. "And now you'd better go."

She smiled up at him, then picked up her purse from the chair, turned, and left the room, triumph striding in her long legs.

When the door had closed, the Man in the Black Hat laughed softly and sat there staring after her.

AT THAT same moment, far out on East Washington Street, Doro Kelly slowed Arthur Henshaw's car at the curb and set the hand-brake. There was enough light from a street lamp so that she could see the depression in the cushion beside her. There was no other visible indication of Captain Zero's presence in the car with her.

"It's no good," she said. "Maria has given us the slip for sure. Those streets back there, who laid them out—a couple of waltzing mice with the double jimjams?"

Zero's invisible eyes worried over her. He said, *"You'd better drop me off downtown somewhere and then head for Pendleville, angel. All this is very ungood. They've got you tagged by now as an associate of Captain Zero. They've got some kind of a radio network,*

I tell you. I heard Maria trying to get through a call before she ducked out of the bathroom window."

She said, "You want me to 'phone the police about the body in Maria's apartment?"

"No," he replied. *"We can't do that. If they take Maria up on a murder charge, there goes my one good lead to the Phi Gang. I haven't got anything except Maria. And I haven't got her, of course. Not now. So you'd better trade off Henshaw's car for your own, get back to Pendleville, and just forget the whole thing."*

Doro Kelly lifted her decisive little chin a bit. "Nuh-uh."

"What do you mean—nuh-uh?"

"I mean that the Kellys never were much good at running away. Except from a banshee. Besides, I'm here on a newspaper assignment."

"Why don't you let Lee Allyn handle the assignment."

"I should say not," she returned hotly. "He's a nice boy, but not much of a reporter. I'm in this thing to the finish and I'll do it."

Zero sighed. *"That's what I'm afraid of—the finish."*

CHAPTER 13
COUNTERSPY

NINE A.M. the following morning, Lee Allyn sat in his hotel room having a cup of coffee along with the latest edition of the *Record*. He had as yet found no mention of a homicide occurring in an apartment leased by Maria Renard. He wondered just how Maria had managed to dispose of the body.

Maybe, he thought with a shudder, she hadn't. Maybe Gil was still there.

As he started to reach for his coffee cup, a short item on page one caught his eye. It was datelined Aztec, New Mexico:

Lee Allyn

> Senator Walter Dunnwoody, who yesterday reported the loss of his guide, is himself missing from his camp in the mountains near here. Luke Meyers, of Aztec, arrived at the Dunnwoody camp late in the evening with supplies—

Allyn's reading was interrupted by a knock at the door. He put the paper down on the writing desk, got up, and crossed the hotel room. Beyond the threshold stood Ed Cavanaugh, chief of the Pendleville police and the last person Allyn would have expected to see in Indianapolis.

With Cavanaugh was a man of medium height, wearing a gray suit and hat, with clean-cut features and lively brown eyes.

"Well, I'll be damned," Lee Allyn said and put out his hand to Cavanaugh who shook it heartily.

"This is Mr. Browne," Cavanaugh introduced the man in the gray suit. That was all—no attempted explanation as to what

127

Mr. Browne did nor why he had been brought to Allyn's room. Mr. Browne's handshake was brief but firm. His lively eyes gave Allyn a complete going over, and then his blunt-fingered hands reached into the inner pocket of his gray suit coat and brought out a series of photographs—all head-and-shoulder shots of a man with light blond hair who wore across the front of his dark shirt a placard about the size of an auto license plate and which bore a series of numbers.

Mr. Browne stared at the photos—which had certainly come out of a rogues' gallery—and then he stared at Lee Allyn. There was nothing on Mr. Browne's face to indicate that everything was fine and dandy.

Allyn glanced uneasily at Cavanaugh. "Hey, what is this? Whose mug is that?"

Cavanaugh didn't say anything, but Browne did.

"It could almost be your mug, Mr. Allyn. Almost, but not quite."

Lee Allyn sighed his relief. "Well, I'm thankful for the small difference."

Nobody else looked thankful. Cavanaugh seemed slightly disappointed.

"Don't you think it will work?" he asked Mr. Browne.

"It might," Browne decided, still staring at Allyn in a manner that did not make for complete relaxation. "It just might work. He's the right height and build. The right complexion. He wouldn't fool Mrs. Taber, but then we're not concerned about that." He nodded. "I think you'll do."

"Well, good for me," Allyn returned, still completely in the dark.

"That is, if what Cavanaugh says of you is true."

Allyn looked anxiously at Ed Cavanaugh who met his gaze squarely. Cavanaugh shook his head slightly in answer to Allyn's silent question: Had Cavanaugh told Browne that Allyn was Captain Zero?

Browne was saying, "I'm the local field officer of the Federal Bureau of Investigation. Cavanaugh has been telling me about you."

"About how you tackled Sam Dawson the other day," Cavanaugh said. He went over to the writing desk, turned the chair about to face the room, and sat down. Allyn pointed out the lounge chair to the FBI and seated himself on the edge of the bed. He looked from one to the other of his visitors.

"So I look like somebody in the rogues' gallery," he said. "So what? I'm all ears."

BROWNE SAID, "Cavanaugh tells me you're a nervy little devil, and I won't think otherwise of you if you turn down the proposition I'm about to make. If you turn it down, I'll just think you're nervy and smart. It's a thankless job and may get yourself killed. On the other hand, you might be able to furnish us with just the break we need to put the Phi Gang people where they belong."

"It's pretty big, isn't it?" Allyn asked. "The Phi Gang, I mean."

"We don't know how big," Browne said grimly. "Big enough to have plenty of money to throw around. And they'll have a lot more if this ransom deal with Mrs. Burton Ivars goes through. A hundred thousand dollars more, at any rate."

Allyn whistled. "That's the asking price?"

Browne nodded. He took from his billfold a piece of note paper which he handed to Allyn. "That came in on one of Roscoe Brun's pigeons early this morning."

Allyn's pale eyes scanned the message.

> Major Brun:
>
> This is our second communication. You may inform Mrs. Burton Ivars that we have priced Mr. Ivars' life at one hundred thousand dollars. She should immediately raise that in cash, in unmarked hundred dollar bills.
>
> You, Major Brun, are to serve as go-between. Our third communication will inform you exactly how this money is to be made available to us. Within twenty-four hours after payment is made, Mr. Burton Ivars will be safely returned home.
>
> Ø
>
> P.S. It has occurred to us that police may be over-exerting themselves in an effort to trace this typewriter. Wishing to spare them as much inconvenience as possible, you may inform them that it is a portable which belonged to the late James Oliver. Since we will have no use for this machine after writing the third communication, police may recover the typewriter from the Water Company canal, if still interested.

Lee Allyn looked up and from Cavanaugh to Browne. "Was there a Phi Gang before Sam Dawson killed James Oliver in Pendleville the other afternoon?"

The FBI man frowned. "Of course. There would have to be. It's too well organized to have sprung up in a short time."

"That's not exactly what I meant. Did the sign—" here Allyn drew an oval in the air and put a diagonal through it—"that Greek letter or whatever it is, did it ever appear prior to the order which Sam Dawson received directing him to kill James Oliver?"

Browne looked at Cavanaugh. Cavanaugh's expression was blank.

"Not as far as I know," he said. "It seems to me that the Pendleville *World* is wholly responsible for the tag the Phi Gang."

Allyn pulled thoughtfully on an ear lobe. "You know there's something funny about that. Doesn't a note scribbled on the margin of a newspaper seem a little crude in comparison to all the evidence we've had as to the efficiency of this mob?

"Consider these notes that have been coming in to Brun's pigeon loft, think of the planning back of all that—the theft of the pigeons, the use of James Oliver's portable. Everything was worked out to the most minute detail a long ways ahead of time. Yet Oliver was murdered on the strength of a directive scribbled on a newspaper margin. There's something makeshift about that. It doesn't fit. To me, it doesn't fit."

"There might have been a last minute change in plans," Browne suggested. "Maybe the script called for somebody else to kill Oliver, but it was finally decided to give Dawson the job."

"Well, it's by me," Cavanaugh admitted. "And I don't think it has much to do with the business at hand, has it, Browne?"

BROWNE AGREED that it didn't. He took out cigarettes

131

which he passed around, and when he had lighted his he came forward to the edge of his chair and addressed Lee Allyn.

"With a crew haircut and some prison clothes, I think you just might pass for John Taber."

"Is that good or bad?" Allyn wanted to know.

"You probably won't consider it a compliment, if that's what you mean," the Federal man said. "Taber is serving time for embezzlement, and we happen to know that he's wanted by the Phi Gang. In fact, he's so badly wanted that he is scheduled to break prison late this afternoon. Don't ask me what the gang wants with a rich man's son who couldn't keep his hands out of the till, but they want him and they're willing to try anything to get him."

"They want him alive, you mean," Cavanaugh put in. "I think the proposition will have more appeal to Allyn if you bring that out."

Browne nodded. "They want him to join their mob, of course," he explained.

"How did you get advance notice on this?" Allyn wanted to know.

"Just a break," Browne admitted. "One of our men noticed a plane flying at night near the prison. He noticed something screwy about the wingtip lights of that plane. Instead of flashing first red and then green—alternating like that—these lights would sometimes flash twice on the red wingtip to maybe one on the green.

"In short, the plane was sending out Morse code, a message intended for John Taber. We've double-checked. Taber, an enthusiastic yachtsman before he was tried and found guilty, knows the code. His cell was in such a location that he could have watched the plane. So for once in our lives we're a jump ahead of the Phi Gang.

"We've got two alternatives," Browne went on hurriedly before Allyn could interrupt. "We can either let Taber think he'll get away with it, and then

Ed Cavanaugh

try to snare the members of the gang used on this particular caper. Or we can substitute somebody for Taber to get into the very core of their organization, get us the necessary information so that we can wipe out the whole mob. Unfortunately for us, Taber is a little bit undersize, according to the standards of the FBI."

"And I'm about Taber's size," Allyn interrupted. "You want me to impersonate Taber, is that it?"

Browne nodded. "And I repeat, I won't think any less of you if you refuse."

ALLYN WAS thoughtfully silent for a moment. Time was what worried him. Browne, of course, did not know that Lee Allyn periodically vanished at midnight and remained invisible until dawn. There might not be time between the hour of the scheduled prison break and midnight for Allyn to accomplish anything. Suppose the getaway scheme called for a lay-over period in some hideout provided by the gang and the criminals discovered they had taken Captain Zero into their midst?

"Well?" Browne smiled at Allyn. "What's the answer?"

"How do we get to the prison?"

"By plane. Within an hour," Browne told him. "You'll be smuggled in, of course, in such a manner that damned few people will know about it. I might also warn you, that damned few will know about the prison break, too. There will be shooting—plenty of the real thing. Your life will be entirely in the hands of the Phi crowd. Up to now they haven't made any mistakes. But—" Browne shrugged eloquently.

"Have I got time to say good-bye to a certain girl?" Allyn asked.

"Time, maybe," Browne said, "but we don't want you to do that. For your own sake, we don't want you to, as much as for ours. This has got to be pulled off on the QT, absolutely."

Allyn hated the idea of simply walking out of Doro Kelly's life, perhaps never to see her again. But perhaps that was the best way after all. Walk out and stay out. She'd eventually get over her dream about Captain Zero. She'd probably begin to realize what a really swell egg Ed Cavanaugh was. Allyn smiled slightly at Cavanaugh.

"Time maybe for a brief last will and testament?"

Cavanaugh looked uneasily at Browne. Browne, apparently a very practical man with no illusions whatever, nodded and said, "I think that's a good idea. We've got a lawyer in the office who'll be glad—"

Allyn was shaking his head. "I haven't anything of value. What I've got I'm leaving to Cavanaugh."

"Huh?" The police chief stared at him.

Allyn laughed, took a pad of paper from his pocket along with a pencil stub. On the top sheet he wrote:

Ed, how would you read this?

Beneath that line he printed in pencil:

10øRANGES

Then in long hand again:

Is it, "Ten ranges," or "one hundred ranges," or only "ten oranges"? Just something I have been meaning to ask a number of people.

Aside from that brainstorm, I have nothing to offer except that Maria Renard, Winston Apartments on Arlington Avenue, is top lady in ø gang.

O not ø

Allyn tore the sheet off the pad, folded it carefully in quarters, handed it to Cavanaugh. "Put that in your pocket, Ed, for sometime when you haven't got anything better to do." Turning to the FBI man, he said, "I'm ready anytime you are."

CHAPTER 14
ALIAS NUMBER THREE

AT 9:45 A.M. Doro Kelly, dressed for the street in her trim black suit and hat, stepped out into the hotel corridor and along it to the room occupied by Lee Allyn. She knocked vigorously but got no answer.

She turned, somewhat piqued that he would slip out without at least stopping to say good-morning, went to the elevator and down into the lobby. There she approached the clerk at the desk.

"Can you tell me what time Mr. Allyn went out this morning?"

"Mr. Allyn checked out about fifteen minutes ago."

"*Checked* out?" she repeated, amazed. "You mean he's left the hotel and is on his way back to Pendleville?"

"Mr. Allyn didn't mention his destination, Miss Kelly," the clerk replied. "But he certainly left the hotel."

Doro, cheeks flushed, turned from the desk and started across the lobby toward the coffee shop. She was both angry and hurt, and anger predominated. That is, she wanted it to predominate.

"The little d-d-d-drip!" she named Mr. Allyn under her breath and blinked burning eyes rapidly.

Over breakfast coffee she formulated a plan. It was, she knew, a desperate, crazy sort of a plan, but then it matched her mood at the moment. She was full of bitterness. Not only was she destined never to see Captain Zero, but now Lee Allyn had heaped disappointment on top of disappointment. They had quarreled before, usually over Lee's insistence on early retirement, but never before had resentment carried over to the following day.

"Hello, Doro."

She glanced up. Ed Cavanaugh was standing on the opposite side of the table, his hand on the back of the chair. His smile didn't seem to alter the wooden-Indian aspect of his face in the least.

"Ed!" she crowed. "What in the world are you doing here? Sit down and tell me about it."

The Pendleville police chief pulled out the chair and sat down. He ordered coffee from the waitress who appeared immediately at his elbow.

"The Ivars kidnaping," he explained quietly when the waitress had left. "The obvious connection between it and the Dawson business in Pendleville. I was on my way to Roscoe Brun's place and thought I'd drop by and say hello."

She said that was nice of him. "What are they doing—the police, I mean?"

Cavanaugh shrugged. "The only thing they can do. They've got a plane up, trying to spot the carrier pigeons. And not having any luck, of course. Too many pigeons in this town. Brun has been named go-between. He seems to relish the job."

CAVANAUGH'S COFFEE arrived. He added four teaspoons of sugar, and while he stirred, his dark eyes stared at the girl who sat opposite him.

Doro asked casually, "Have you seen Lee Allyn this morning?"

"No," Cavanaugh said, his eyes steady. "Why?"

"No reason, particularly."

Cavanaugh tasted his coffee and added more sugar. "Like to go out to Brun's with me?"

"And do what?"

He shrugged. "Watch for the third and last pigeon. That's all there is to do. Mrs. Ivars has the ransom money all ready to pass over to Brun just as soon as the third communication explains how and where the money is to be paid."

"Are they going to get away with it—the gang, I mean?"

Cavanaugh said, "Don't know. Local police and the Feds can't plan much of a counter-offensive until those final instructions come through, and my guess is that the third communication will insist upon delivery of the money immediately, which won't give the law much chance to rig a trap."

Doro had finished her coffee. "I don't think I'll go with you, Ed," she said slowly. "The idea of just sitting around in Brun's pigeon loft waiting for that bird to show up impresses me as being just a wee bit futile. I think I'll just—" she paused—"well, maybe I'll be around later. Right now I've got to do some shopping." She smiled at him. " 'Bye for now."

She walked across the coffee shop to the street entrance, trying not to hurry. Once outside, she walked by the front of the coffee shop, noted that Cavanaugh was still at the table, and re-entered the hotel lobby. She took the elevator up to her room which she entered and went straight to the small suitcase which stood on the luggage stand at the foot of the bed.

As she began to unpack the contents, her pulse quickened. She was on the threshold of danger. She sought it, craved it as a counter-irritant for disappointment. And where there was danger she was likely to find Captain Zero.

She removed the entire contents of the suitcase except the small, heavy object wrapped in white cotton flannel. This was a small caliber revolver which Ed Cavanaugh himself had given her two years ago when she had taken up police reporting. That done, she closed the case, carried it to the door and out into the hall.

Doro went from the hotel to a nearby department store where she bought a pair of man-tailored gray gabardine slacks. She then took an elevator to the men's clothing department where, under the pretext of outfitting her non-existent husband, she bought a topcoat, a scarf, a gray felt hat, and the smallest pair of brown oxfords in stock. These she packed into her suitcase.

By offering suitable identification, she was able to pay for her purchases by check. The hundred dollars in cash she had in her purse she was saving for still another purchase—the most important one of them all.

She went to the corner drugstore where she accumulated a pair of plain sun-glasses and a slim cigar which the clerk assured her was exceedingly mild. And then from there to a jewelry store which displayed hearing aids in the window.

If the man who had driven the getaway truck for the gang in Pendleville wore a hearing aid and if Maria Renard did also Doro was convinced that hearing aids had something to do with the manner in which the Phi Gang operated. While it could scarcely be a badge, it might serve as such for a brief moment. What she actually suspected was that the hearing aids used by the Phi Gang were something quite different from the one which she purchased for ninety-five dollars—a model with a black plastic case and black, bone conduction receiver.

"I'm not hard of hearing," she felt called upon to explain. "It's for my uncle, a birthday present. Then if it doesn't work for him, or if he needs a different kind, you'll be glad to make an exchange, won't you?"

The clerk said he'd be delighted. She managed to talk him out of wrapping the hearing aid as a gift, hurried from the store, and caught a taxi which took her out East Washington Street as far as Arlington.

A MINUTE later she was in the ladies' rest room of a filling station where she removed her black suit, her slip, her hat, and high-heeled pumps. She scrubbed every trace of makeup from her face, yet the flush of excitement was not vastly different from her rouge. She put on the newly purchased slacks and oxfords, and what with the frilly blouse she had on, she still looked feminine. But then that was all right for now, she decided.

She pinned up her short dark curls on the top of her head, put on sun-glasses and then the gray felt hat. And now, the mirror told her, she looked slightly nuts. The hat was responsible. It was completely masculine, and it was going to take nerve to walk out of the women's room with that on her head.

She put on the hearing aid, the ear piece in its proper place, the black plastic case temporarily pinned to the front of her blouse. She packed her feminine attire away in the suitcase, put the loaded revolver, the cigar, and the scarf into the pocket of the topcoat.

"Doro, you *are* nuts!" she said to herself, and a final glance in the mirror verified this. Without the hat and with the frilly blouse exposed, she probably could have left the station without attracting any great amount of attention. But now—

She drew a long breath, picked up the suitcase, and threw the topcoat over her arm.

The station attendant had a customer at the gas pumps, for which Doro was grateful. Metal clatter plates on the heels of the masculine oxfords seemed to scream, "Look at me, everybody. I'm nuts!" She didn't run but she wanted to.

The conversation between the station attendant and his customer broke off suddenly, and Doro knew that they had sighted her. She didn't even glance at them but hurried out into the street, conscious that people in the cars that rolled swiftly by were noticing her.

She turned into Arlington, and by the time she had gone a block, her shoes were killing her. They were too big in every direction and they rubbed. She was developing a limp which, she thought, might turn out to be a blessing in disguise. It would perhaps help conceal her feminine carriage.

When she was out of sight of the filling station, she put her suitcase down on the sidewalk, dug the scarf out of the topcoat pocket, put it around her neck and spread it as widely as possible to hide the front of her blouse.

Across the street from where she stood, a woman was sweeping her front porch with at least half an eye on Doro. Ahead of her, the driver of a bakery truck paused with a basket on his arm to stare at her.

Doro set her teeth, jammed her arms into the sleeves of the gray topcoat. Before she buttoned the coat and turned up its collar, she brought the case of the hearing aid out into the open and fastened it to a lapel. It was rather a shapeless coat, and she hoped that now that she was inside it, she too was shapeless.

She limped on, beyond the stares of the housewife and baker's boy. She noticed to her satisfaction that she was attracting practically no attention from passing motorists. When she came within sight of the Winston Apartments she completed her disguise with the slim cigar which she clenched in her teeth but did not light.

Now, she thought, she had a fairly decent chance of gaining admission into Maria Renard's apartment. After that—what? She didn't know. Let the circumstances decide.

DORO HAD been counting on the telegram ruse she and Zero had employed the previous night as a means of getting past the electric lock on the front door of the building. But here she got an unlooked-for break. As she approached the door from the outside, a man with a briefcase showed up in the foyer, apparently on his way to the office and in a great hurry.

He pushed the door open, scarcely seemed to notice Doro who passed in as he went out. Without pausing to think—lest thinking spoil the fine edge of her courage—she hurried up the stairs, the three full flights, and now stood, breathless and shaking, in front of the door of C-3.

THE FRANTIC quality of her knock was not all assumed. She kept knocking until she heard the whisper of footsteps beyond the panel.

Maria's voice asked, "Who is it?"

"Hurry!" Doro stage-whispered. "Let me in, Number Three."

As Maria twisted the lock, Doro turned her head somewhat to the left so that the black button of the hearing aid was very much in evidence. In the pocket of her topcoat, her hand clutched the butt of the small revolver. The door was opened a cautious eight inches. Doro saw Maria's oval, ivory-hued face, her green eyes shiny with alarm; saw the vivid splash of scarlet that was Maria's satin lounge robe.

Doro put a shoulder to the edge of the door and pushed suddenly and with everything she had. At the same time, she whispered, "Zero is on his way here. I was to warn you!"

And then she was in. She was leaning back against the door to shut it. She was jerking the revolver from the pocket of her topcoat, and only then did she look directly at Maria.

Maria took a gasping breath. Her eyes widened with alarm and immediately narrowed. Her right hand started creeping up toward her bosom, and it was then that Doro noticed that the other woman wore earrings that were like large gold buttons. Only a little while before, in the jewelry store, Doro had seen a hearing aid the receiver of which was matched by a gold earring.

"Keep both hands down at your sides, Maria!" Doro warned, her voice shrill.

Maria dropped her hands. Her eyes were slits and her lips curved into a superior smile.

"Why, it's the girl reporter from Pendleville," she said.

"Turn around." Doro ordered. And when that didn't bring any results, she pushed the muzzle of the revolver into Maria's tummy directly beneath her shapely bosom. The gun found something hard where there should have been only softness— it was the concealed case of the hearing aid. Doro now firmly believed it was not a hearing aid at all but some sort of a compact radio device.

"Turn around," she repeated, "and keep your hands down and in sight. One move toward that radio you're packing, and I'll shoot."

Maria shrugged and turned. "But don't you think that you might become involved with the police?" she asked. "There are laws against armed assault and murder—or haven't you heard?"

The implication was as clear as if she had said, "You haven't got a thing on me, and if you were to shoot they'd hang you for murder." Which was perfectly true. Had the police walked into the room right then, there would have been no question as to which of the two women to arrest. There was no possible charge which could have been pinned on Maria. Yet she stood high in the organization of the most ruthless criminal gang ever to terrorize a free nation.

Doro said, "Never mind that. Just walk toward the bedroom. If you think I'd hesitate to shoot, you might try something." She kept the gun close to, but not touching, Maria's back as they moved toward the door of the bedroom. When Maria was within a step of the threshold, Doro clenched her teeth, gripped the gun by barrel and cylinder, brought the butt of it up high and down on top of Maria's head.

It was a good blow, but it wasn't good enough. Maria, partially stunned, staggered and dropped down on one knee at the same

144

time emitting a sharp, hurt cry. She put both hands up to the top of her head, and there wasn't anything Doro could do except swing and hit her again.

The blow was lower and it carried everything that Doro could possibly muster. Maria went all the way down to the floor, face to the carpet, her arms extended above her head.

Doro dropped the revolver into her pocket. She sidled through the door to avoid stepping on Maria, stooped, got hold of Maria's arms, and dragged the other woman to the bed.

"I don't know why," she muttered. "I don't know why I ought to put you on the bed. Except that leaving you on the floor looks so damned careless."

So she got Maria up onto the bed, and then immediately zipped open the front of the scarlet lounge robe the woman wore, revealing what appeared to be the white plastic case of a hearing aid fastened to the front of Maria's slip. Doro got the plastic case off, followed the thin wire up to the gold button which Maria had fastened to her right ear. Doro got the button off, not caring much what happened to Maria's ear.

HER HANDS trembling, Doro fastened the gold button to her own ear and studied the plastic case in her hand. There was a switch on it exactly like the real hearing aid which Doro herself had purchased. In the present position of the switch, Doro could hear a faint hum from the receiver fastened to her earlobe. When she pushed the switch into its alternate position, the hum stopped.

Suppose it actually was a hearing aid? Suppose she'd guessed wrong about the whole thing?

Doro put the switch back to its original position. There was the hum again and suddenly a short, sharp musical tone that was like a time signal on the radio.

Her heart bounded up into her throat. A signal of some sort coming from the gold button receiver of the device. How did she answer? Was it intended for Maria, and if so, what ought she to do?

The signal came again, and then she was listening to an emotionless, metallic voice that seemed to come from a vast distance.

"Calling Three. Calling Three. GHQ calling Three. Come in Sector Officer Three. Standing by."

The signal again, and then only the hum.

Now what? What did she do? Number Three was Maria. Maria was supposed to "come in." Come in where? How?

She fumbled with the plastic case, would have dropped it to the floor except for the wire connecting it to the dingus on her ear. That peeping signal again, and the metallic voice repeated:

"Calling Number Three. This is GHQ calling Three. Come in, Three."

Doro moved the switch. "Hel—" she began. No, that wasn't right. That wasn't the way it should be done. This wasn't a telephone and you didn't say hello. "This is Three," she said faintly, the case close to her mouth. "Calling GHQ and standing by."

She popped the switch into its previous position. At once the metallic spoke to her.

"Number Three, you will be joined by Number Seven in thirty minutes. All arrangements for procedure have been made with Number Seven. He is five-eleven, one hundred sixty-five pounds, thirty-five, gray eyes, light brown hair, wearing brown suit, red tie. He will be carrying a paper shopping bag. A paper shopping bag. You will be ready to move at that time. All clear, Number Three?"

Doro got the switch back to the transmitting position. "All clear."

All clear as mud, she thought and snapped the switch.

There was nothing more from GHQ except the high-pitched electrical note which was possibly used to designate beginning and end of the transmission.

Doro let the white plastic case dangle. She stared at the unconscious Maria on the bed. Why had GHQ described Number Seven? Was it that Number Seven and Maria had not yet met? If the answer to this was yes—

Doro scrambled onto the edge of the bed and studied Maria's face. They were, she had previously noted, approximately the same height, Maria being perhaps a little heavier. The coloring of Maria's skin was vastly different from that of any woman that Doro had ever seen, much paler than her own and with a slight yellowish cast. But both she and Maria had dark hair.

As for the eyes, Doro's varied from blue to green, depended a good deal on what she wore. If she could find something in Maria's wardrobe that was green, something that she could wear to accent the greenish lights in her own eyes—even a string of vivid green beads would do it. If she could in some manner palm herself off on Number Seven as Number Three, she'd be in on the inside of the Phi Gang.

147

She bounced from the bed, began hopping about on one foot while she untied the laces of one of the torturous oxfords she wore.

"I'll try it!" she said aloud. "I'll try anything once!"

She kicked the oxford off, stood with one shoe on, and wondered what she was going to do about Maria. How could she keep Maria out of the picture while she, Doro, was playing her rôle as Number Three?

And then she remembered that somewhere she had read what an effective straightjacket a wet sheet could be. She'd strip Maria, roll her tightly in a wet sheet, and bind her with anything and everything that was handy. And use a gag which, if Maria choked on it, would be just a little bit all right.

She glanced at her watch. It was then 10:12. She had twenty-eight minutes in which to dispose of Maria and dress herself in time to expect Number Seven's knock at the door.

CHAPTER 15
THE LAST COMMUNICATION

AT 10:20 A.M. a pigeon alighted on the ledge outside one of the arched openings in the loft of the old house belonging to Roscoe Brun. Ed Cavanaugh, seated in a folding chair on the inner side of the wire mesh partition, saw it first and nudged the heavy-set, gray-templed plainclothesman beside him. Cavanaugh didn't say anything.

Detective-Lieutenant Sarcoff of the Indianapolis police

glanced toward the arched opening and nodded. Not until the bird had hopped on into its cage did Sarcoff move.

"I wonder if they spotted that one," he said as he got up from his chair.

"If they didn't, they never will," Cavanaugh said. "This is the third and last, isn't it?"

Sarcoff opened the screened door in the partition, went to the pigeon cage, reached in through the little trap door, and caught the bird. From one of its tail feathers he detached a small cylinder of goose quill which he slit open to remove a rolled strip of paper.

He came back through the partition, closed the door after him, and spread out the piece of onion-skin. Cavanaugh stood beside the Indianapolis cop and looked over the latter's shoulder to read:

Major Brun:
This is our third communication.

At 4:00 P.M. you will park your car at the top of the hill over-looking Little Eagle Creek on what is known as Grayson Road six and one half miles northwest of Flackville.

You will then walk down the road and to the concrete bridge which spans the stream. The sign ø in chalk marks a rough ledge on the pile of the bridge span, beneath the arch. You will leave the money on that ledge.

Under no circumstances is anyone except you, Major Brun, to approach within five hundred yards of this from the hour of 4:00 to 5:00. We therefore suggest that if the police are truly interested in preventing murder—in this case, the murder of Burton Ivars—that they barricade this portion of the road to all cars except yours.

Burton Ivars will be released in twenty-four hours from the time the money is in our hands—provided instructions are carried out to the letter.

Ø

"The brass guts of 'em!" Sarcoff said. "We're to barricade the road for 'em! By damn, that's not all we'll do. We'll have the best telephoto lenses in the business trained on that bridge."

"Where's Brun right now?"

Sarcoff looked at his watch. "He ought to be here with Mrs. Ivars and Mr. Nolan."

"Nolan?" Cavanaugh repeated. "That Reg Nolan, the lawyer?"

Sarcoff nodded. "Damned sporting of them to give us until four o'clock to get set. I figured that when it came through it would be one of those hurry-up things."

"They're being sporting," Cavanaugh said dryly, "because they're cocksure of getting away with it. And I'll tell you this, Sarcoff, if you catch a picture of anybody approaching the bridge to pick up that ransom money, that's all you'll ever have—just a picture. You'll be able to use it to identify a corpse in the morgue—that's all."

SARCOFF FOLDED the ransom note carefully. "You think if we get a picture, that guy's a dead duck, huh?"

Cavanaugh nodded. "They'll kill him to keep him from talking. They just don't give a damn. Look what they did to James Oliver when he was playing the game their way."

"We've got to have a try at it though."

"Sure," Cavanaugh agreed. "Only don't get optimistic about the possibilities of snaring the kidnapers through any tele-photo stunts. Incidentally, how does Brun feel about it? How does he know there won't be somebody under the bridge ready to knock him off?

"That's been pulled on the go-between before, you know. It's not a bad trick because the police eyes see one guy go in and one guy come out, and they don't realize until it's too late that the one who comes out isn't the go-between."

Sarcoff grunted. "If they try that on the Major they may have a small war on their hands. I served under him in the first World War. He's not all spit and polish. He's got his share of guts, old Roscoe has."

Cavanaugh followed Sarcoff from the loft and down the two flights of stairs at the foot of which stood Brun's old servant.

"The Major has just returned, sir," the servant announced. "He's in the library." He conducted them to the door of the tall, book-walled room, and even before they had entered they could hear Brun calling the Phi Gang names.

"Damned blackguards, that's what they are!" Brun turned to the door, his blunt dark eyes jabbing at the two police. "Hello there. Any news? That third bird hasn't come in yet, has it?"

Sarcoff nodded, reached into his pocket for the ransom note. He smiled sympathetically at the tall, handsome woman of forty who was seated on the leather upholstered sofa, a small paper-wrapped parcel clutched tightly in gloved hands.

Mrs. Ivars, Cavanaugh presumed. The woman's eyes were

darkly circled, her lips tightly compressed as though to stop their trembling. Standing beside her was Reg Nolan, the attorney, silent and sullen-eyed.

Brun began to read the ransom note aloud, pausing every other sentence to define the Phi Gang in profane terms.

"That doesn't help much, Roscoe," Nolan's deep voice interrupted. "We know what they are. Just read the note and keep your comments to yourself, can't you?"

"What? Ah?" Brun looked at Nolan. "But they've got my dander up, damn them. I feel helpless." He wheeled suddenly to Sarcoff. "Your spotters, man? Is it possible they may have seen the pigeon? There's not much smog this morning."

Sarcoff stepped to the 'phone on Brun's desk and dialed a number. The room listened.

"Sarcoff talking. Anything from the plane?"

The room kept listening. Sarcoff frowned heavily, put the handset down with a sigh. He shook his head, moved over to the doorway where Cavanaugh stood.

"No damned good, Ed. No damned good at all."

Mrs. Ivars said, "I don't care about catching them. Nothing matters really, just so Burt gets back alive." She was close to tears.

Cavanaugh backed out of the library with Sarcoff following him. Cavanaugh said, "I'll get out of your hair now until about three or three-thirty. I'd like to be counted in then, though."

Sarcoff nodded. "You know where to meet me. The Feds have the telephoto cameras. Everything'll be set up by then." His voice dropped to a whisper. "I just hope to heaven Ivars is alive, that's all. The rats won't be running any greater risk if they knocked him off, and it might be considerably more convenient for them."

Cavanaugh, guided by the servant, went to the front door and out into the spring sunshine. He walked southward toward the nearest bus stop, taking it slow, his dark eyes on the ground, his hands in his pockets.

When he got to the corner, he paused, took from his pocket the slip of paper which Lee Allyn had given him. Last will and testament, Allyn had called it. He'd said, "I'm leaving everything I've got to Cavanaugh."

Major Roscoe Brun

Cavanaugh opened the paper and read the note over three times. Most of it didn't make sense—the part about the ranges and oranges. But the business about Maria Renard made sense. That Cavanaugh could do something about.

AT EXACTLY 10:45 Doro Kelly heard a knock at the door of Maria Renard's apartment. She'd been anticipating it, which possibly heightened its effect upon her. She sat bolt upright in the chair, the green taffeta hostess gown which she wore rustling in alarm.

Maria Renard was in the bathtub, not taking a bath. She was

still unconscious and she was swathed in a wet sheet which, in turn, was securely bound and knotted with a strong nylon cord Doro had found in the bathroom.

Doro started toward the door, paused a moment to glance at herself in the mirror. She didn't look like Maria—thank heaven—but she did appear to have green eyes. And her hair was black—black and short, whereas Maria's was black and long, a slight difference which she hoped to be able to take care of. She wore Maria's heavy gold ear buttons, one of which was the receiver of the hearing-aid radio device.

The knock at the door was repeated. Doro's hand went to the knob, hesitated a moment before she turned it over and pulled the door open a little way.

The man took off his hat. His light gray, expressionless eyes seemed inconsistent with his wavy brown hair. She noted the brown paper shopping bag he carried in his right hand and the black hearing aid he wore.

"I'm looking for apartment number three," he said.

"This—this is it," Doro faltered. "I'm Number Three and you—you're Number Seven?" She looked him in the eye.

He nodded slightly without taking his eyes from her face. Doro opened the door fully. He came in—he and his shopping bag—a man in a brown suit that was too short, with some of the aspects of a country bumpkin which did not extend to those too worldly, up-to-no-good eyes of his. He closed the door, stepped away from it to view her from another angle. He didn't miss anything with those gray eyes, and his smile was one of appreciation.

154

"Black Hat didn't over rate you, baby," he said without moving his lips much.

"You should know," she said coldly. She crossed to Maria's coffee table, picked up a cigarette box which she passed to him. He took one, and they both got lights off the same kitchen match.

"What's the caper this time?" she wanted to know and noticed, in a quick rush of panic, that his gaze lingered on her hair which was black and short and curled, whereas Maria's was long and straight. She put a hand to the back of her hair and fluffed out her short bob.

"I can't get used to it," she said. "I just had it cut and waved." She forced a laugh that tinkled with nervousness. "Like it?"

"I'd like to run my fingers through it," he said softly, "but that's a pleasure that'll have to come after business. We've got to move. We're going north by private plane. We've got to fill in a link of the getaway chain for a guy who's going to break out of stir."

Doro's eyelids closed to hide the alarm she felt would show in them. A prison break! She couldn't imagine anything more dangerous, nor anything in which she would be more completely helpless.

"It's a shame to spoil the effect," Number Seven was saying, "but you've got to make up like an old woman—my dear old mother."

She opened her eyes and found him extending the shopping bag to her.

"There's the junk you'll have to put on," he told her. "And you're to carry the bag—just been to town for a day of haggling with the merchants, see? Better pack a rod in it, just in case we run into anything rough. And you're not deaf, see?" He tapped the plastic case fastened to the front of his suit coat. "I'm the one who's deaf, baby."

She understood. "You're to give the orders." She took the shopping bag from his hand, worked her lips into a smile. "Just sit down, big boy, while I make a hag out of myself."

He moved to a chair. "That'll take some hard doing, baby."

SHE CARRIED the bag into the bedroom, closed the door, and on second thought propped a chair beneath the doorknob. She began unpacking the bag—faded pink cotton dress, black shoes with run-over cuban heels, heavy black lisle stockings, a threadbare gray coat, a blue felt hat with a veil and ornamented with a bunch of seed catalogue cherries, a yellowish gray wig.

She stared at the heap which was to constitute her disguise and reflected that she was probably the only girl in the world who never at any time had entertained the slightest desire to go on the stage. Her histrionic ability was absolutely nil. There was still time to give the whole thing up. She could go into the bathroom, take the nylon cord off the unconscious Maria, tie it to the radiator, and make her getaway.

Or could she? There were the dead faces haunting her again with their mute appeal, and now her own had joined them. If she ran away, it was only a matter of time before the tentacles of the Phi Gang would reach for her. She was in this thing up to her ears, and the only thing to do was to see it through.

The thought that death could not be much worse than a short span of life spent running from a gang of murderers steadied her fingers, and she opened the zipper closing of Maria's green taffeta hostess gown.

Twenty minutes later Number Seven tapped on the door of Maria's bedroom. Doro, seated in front of the dressing table mirror, jerked around.

"What is it?" she demanded sharply.

"Just that right now we ought to be on our way out of here, baby. We're running behind schedule."

"Why didn't you tell when the deadline was?" she said crossly and leaned closer to the mirror to sketch cross-feet wrinkles at the corners of her eyes with a dark gray makeup pencil.

"That's all right, baby," his voice came soothingly from behind the door. "Just don't waste any time, that's all. We'll make up whatever we've lost at the other end of the line."

Doro put on the hat with the plaster cherries. She pulled the veil down over her face and pinned the ends of it into that portion of the gray wig which showed at the back of her neck. She stood and put on the shapeless old gray coat.

Now for the shopping bag—something that would enable her to make a bulky package in a hurry. She got the man's topcoat, which she had bought earlier in the day, from Maria's closet, wrapped it in brown paper, stuffed it into the bag. Then her revolver. This she thrust down next to the side of the bag, beneath it and the package.

She clutched the twisted paper handles of the bag in her left hand, limped to the door. The limp would have to be a part of the disguise; not only were there blisters to consider, brought on

Doro backed away
to the door.

by her wearing the masculine oxfords, but the run-over cuban heels of the shoes she now wore twisted her ankles.

She pushed the chair aside, got a hand to the doorknob, hunched her shoulders as she opened the door and faced Number Seven's scrutiny. He looked her over.

Henshaw
rushed at her.

"Well, son," she said in a cracked voice, "you want to take that there airship ride now?"

His laugh was not necessarily a laugh. "Maybe you'd better just keep your mouth shut. That sounded as phony as a lead quarter."

They went to the front door of the apartment and out. They moved toward the stairway, and Number Seven took her arm. They went down, and on the second flight Number Seven steered her close to the railing to make room for a tall man who was ascending—a man whose angular features suggested a carving in some dark wood.

Police Chief Ed Cavanaugh passed with scarcely a glance. And on Doro's arm the hand of Number Seven was like a manacle of steel.

THAT AFTERNOON Lee Allyn, his hair crew-cut and wearing the drab garb of a prisoner, sat on the bunk in the cell that had been allotted to John Taber, convicted embezzler. Money and wire-pulling had brought little homelike touches to Taber's cell.

There were curtains at the barred window—a window through which two nights before, Taber must have watched the flashing red and green wingtip lights of a plane code—a message laden with hope of escape. There was a small radio and a shelf of books—Janes' *Ships,* a volume on navigation, another devoted to historic naval battle maneuvers.

As Allyn's pale eyes ran across the titles of the books, as he recalled that Taber was an enthusiastic and experienced sailor, a fantastic thought began to form in Allyn's brain. A thought so laden with terrible portent that it brought with it a creeping chill along his spine....

While in far-off New Mexico a shadow fell across a flat ledge, high in the Rockies, where the lost Senator Dunnwoody crouched beside a tiny trickle of pure water with which he intended to wash down a dry wholewheat biscuit, the last morsel of his rations.

The Senator looked up, scarcely able to believe his eyes as another, much younger man stepped onto the ledge.

"Th-thank God!" the senator stammered. He straightened up, not now conscious of the pains that knifed his legs nor the burden of utter weariness across his back and shoulders. He stumbled toward the other man, caught powerful upper arms in trembling hands, almost sobbing.

"Thank God!" he said again. And there were tears of joy in his eyes. They'd found him finally. They'd get him out of here. A few days of rest in the hospital and he'd be right as rain again, ready to go back to Washington, back to work. That was what had troubled him even more than a personal reluctance to end his life in this barren wilderness. He *had* to get back to Washington.

As chairman of the committee that would have to pass on the Eastern Seaboard Electrical Power Project, his vote and his alone stood in the way of a scheme which he felt would not only put the government in competition with private enterprise but would also create a political pork barrel that would cost the taxpayers millions upon millions of dollars.

The younger man stood with legs wide-spread and let the

senator paw him to make sure he was a thing of flesh and blood and not an illusion brought on by near starvation.

"Yeah, thank God I found you, Senator," he said less fervently, and fell back a pace.

"Where are the others? The rest of the search party?" the Senator asked.

The other shrugged. "I'm it." He reached in under his tan, weather-proof jacket and brought out a heavy caliber automatic. He worked the slide deliberately, then looked up at the bewildered unshaven face of the ragged man in front of him.

"What—what—who are you?" Senator Dunnwoody stammered, his face slack.

The other laughed coldly. "The name is Childers, though I don't expect you to believe that—not with this face I'm wearing."

"Childers?" the senator repeated mechanically and eyed the heavy gun that was now eyeing him.

"Yeah. That's right. 'The Chill,' they call me. Maybe you can guess why that's what they call me."

The Senator's eyes flicked across the other's face then dropped again to stare in fascination at the automatic.

"But—but why? You're not going to— Look, I'm Senator Dunnwoody. There must be some mistake. I'm Senator Dunnwoody, and I'm lost."

"Yeah," the man whose name was Childers said. "You're lost all right. You're going to stay that way, too."

The blast of the gun hammered against the sheer face of rock and bounded across the chasm, reverberated there, went roistering off to lose itself among the mountains.

Sound and the Senator were dead.

CHAPTER 16
BLOOD MONEY

UNABLE TO get any answer to his knocking on Maria Renard's door, Cavanaugh left the apartment and returned to his hotel. He had an early lunch, then went up to his room where he lay on the bed, fully dressed, and again read the "last will and testament" of Lee Allyn. He still couldn't make any sense out of the business of ranges versus oranges.

He put the paper aside and lay there staring at the ceiling. He was worried. He was chiefly worried about Lee Allyn. If Allyn were to die his much more capable prototype, Captain Zero, died with him. And Zero had become Cavanaugh's own most potent weapon against crime. Now that he looked back upon the move he had made, or that he had urged Browne of the FBI to make, it seemed like an excellent way to waste valuable ammunition.

Then there was a personal side to it that bothered Cavanaugh even more. If anything happened to Allyn it might appear as though Cavanaugh had made the move deliberately to rid himself of what he considered the only stumbling block between him and Doro Kelly.

And if Doro learned that he was the one who had suggested that Allyn take Taber's place to worm his way into their gang, Doro would hold it against Cavanaugh for the rest of her life.

The Allyn substitution was one of those schemes which had

looked very good in the beginning but which now, in the cold light of retrospect, looked pretty mouldy.

"I must be nuts," Cavanaugh grumbled to himself as his mind conjured up a picture of slight, rather frail Lee Allyn pitted against the blazing guns of the Phi Gang.

At three P.M. he got up, brushed some of the wrinkles out of his suit, left the hotel, and walked to police headquarters on Alabama Street where he met his friend Lieutenant Sarcoff. A department car and its police-uniformed driver stood ready, and Cavanaugh and Sarcoff got in and headed for the northwest limits of the city where Roscoe Brun was to make the ransom payment to the Phi Gang.

Eventually, the police car turned into a lane before a farm house situated well back from the road.

"We've got to hike across open country now," Sarcoff explained. "The Feds have got a sweet set-up overlooking the bridge. You'll see what I mean when we get there."

Cavanaugh got out of the car, and he and the Indianapolis cop climbed a fence and started across a broad open pasture where cattle were grazing. The sky above was blue and cloudless, the air calm. Nothing in the immediate vicinity offered any sort of a hiding place, yet Cavanaugh had an uneasy feeling that they were being watched. Imagination, of course. It was simply that the Phi Gang seemed to be everywhere at once.

When they had climbed still another fence, Sarcoff raised a thick arm and pointed west.

"See it, Ed?"

"It" was a shelter for cattle made by piling straw over rude posts and decking to form a kind of cavern.

"That overlooks Little Eagle Creek," Sarcoff explained, "which at this time of the year, with all the rain we've had, isn't exactly little. The Feds have got a telephoto camera in there. If anybody, but anybody, approaches that bridge from any direction, they'll snap a pix that'll blow up life-size."

"Suppose," Cavanaugh suggested pessimistically, "that the gang sends somebody swimming downstream to pick up the ransom haul? That's the first thing that came into my mind when I thought of the set-up as outlined in that last communication." SARCOFF AGREED that this was a possibility. It was something that had occurred to him also. "Nobody can stay under water forever, even with some sort of an air tube that could be kept above the surface. I've got men posted all along the creek, both sides, in strategic places."

Cavanaugh had no comment. He could not help but feel that the key, if there was a key, was a long ways from the bank of Little Eagle, in the northern part of the state where a slight, pale young man awaited liberation from prison by the Phi Gang.

The straw-covered cattle shelter was, as Sarcoff had said, ideally situated. From the tunneled look-out holes in the thick straw wall there was a view of the road and the gently sloping pasture land to the edge of the swollen stream.

Little Eagle was far out of its banks, a racing muddy torrent that broke against the boles of willow and sycamore trees that in summer would have had only reaching rootlets in the water. The bridge was a low, concrete arch, and this was the target of the telephoto camera which the federal men had camouflaged with straw.

Promptly at 4:00, a green sedan came into view along the twisting road. It drove slowly to the top of the hill overlooking the creek and there pulled onto the shoulder beneath a tree.

"That's Major Brun," Sarcoff told Cavanaugh.

Brun got out of the car, a stocky figure, natty in tan gabardine. Cavanaugh, in a straw tunnel with Sarcoff, picked up a pair of binoculars and focused them

Maria Renard

on Roscoe Brun as the latter started down the hill toward the bridge.

Cavanaugh asked, "Does Brun know the set-up here?"

Sarcoff said, "I don't think so. He knows, of course, we've got a telephoto planted somewhere, but we've kept the details pretty well within the official family."

Cavanaugh scanned the bridge with the glasses. Shadows beneath the concrete arch were too deep to penetrate, or perhaps it was simply the angle of his vision. He stared at the arch, trying to penetrate its depth, until his eyes ached with the strain. He was somewhat startled when something drifted out into the open from those shadows and continued on downstream. Something that was nothing, of no significance whatever. It looked like a portion of an old orange crate.

"That reminds me," Cavanaugh said. He put down the glasses which Sarcoff immediately picked up. Cavanaugh took out a pencil and an old envelope, rested the latter on the packed ledge of straw in front of them. With the pencil he printed:

10ØRANGES

He nudged Sarcoff. "How would you read that—one hundred ranges, ten ranges, or only ten oranges?" He held it out.

Sarcoff, plainly annoyed, lowered the glasses and glanced at the envelope. Only a glance, and then he immediately went back to watching Roscoe Brun.

"Ten oranges," Sarcoff answered. "Brun is at the end of the bridge new."

Cavanaugh grunted, pushed the envelope back into the inner pocket of his coat, and stared at the distant figure of Roscoe Brun, clearly silhouetted against the concrete face of the bridge abutment. Clutching the packet of ransom money in his left hand, Brun cautiously made his way down the short steep slope toward the edge of the racing water.

He slipped. Both feet went out from under him, and he skidded on the seat of his pants to stop within inches of the creek. Now he stood in a crouch, peered into the arch of the bridge span, into the shadows beyond. Slowly, cautiously, he inched his way along to disappear in the heavy shadows.

It seemed an eternity before Brun's head emerged from the arch, then shoulders, thick torso, and legs.

"Got his feet wet, didn't he?" Sarcoff said with a short, nervous laugh.

BRUN'S TAN trousers were dark and wet to the knees. He scrambled up the steep bank, clutching at the side of the abutment, gained the approach of the bridge and then the gravel of the road. There he turned around, stared back at the bridge and the rushing water for a moment before starting back toward his car. He kept glancing over his shoulder at intervals all the way to the top of the hill.

As for Sarcoff, he kept the binoculars focused on the bridge and its immediate surroundings.

He said, "We've got a whole damned hour of this. That's what I hate—waiting."

Cavanaugh's laugh was dry. "You mean you hate police work. Half of it's just waiting."

"Don't I know it!"

That was what they did for an hour—waited and watched. And in the straw tunnel next to theirs, the Federal men waited and watched. Cavanaugh could hear the click of the telephoto camera every time any piece of flotsam drifted into and under the bridge. There was plenty of that, mostly heavy branches of trees, old stumps that had finally been uprooted after withstanding the floods of many previous years.

"Anything like that," Sarcoff said as a hoary sycamore log drifted out from beneath the bridge. "Their pick-up man could be clinging to something like that. And there's not a damned thing that isn't going to be photographed and checked. Somewhere along the stream it'll be checked."

He kept talking like that. It seemed to help him wait—the idea that somehow, someway they would get a lead.

Finally, Cavanaugh said, "It's five. On the nose."

"Give 'em ten minutes more," Sarcoff said. "We can't run any risk, if their watches and ours aren't synchronized. We want Ivars to come through alive, above everything. That boy is big stuff, and he's going to be a hell of a lot bigger when he goes to Washington as Secretary of the Treasury."

So they allowed ten more minutes, and then Sarcoff, Cavanaugh, and the two Federal men came out of their hiding place into the open field and took the direct and diagonal route down the long slope toward the bridge. At the same time, Roscoe Brun, who must have sighted them, left his car and started toward the same objective but along the road. By ambling slowly he managed to meet the four officials at the foot of the bridge.

Brun was visibly fuming, his frown a black V between smudgy eyebrows. "That's a hell of a place to get to," he said. "A hell of a place. Look at my pants, will you? Ripped the seat, and then finally slipped into the drink after I got under the bridge."

Nobody was interested in Brun's pants. Sarcoff and one of the Feds were already on their way down the steep slope. The latter slipped as Brun had done, landed with his left leg in the water. Sarcoff, older and perhaps more careful, had better luck. Cavanaugh and the others waited beside the abutment.

"It's not easy to find that ledge under there," Brun shouted to the men beneath the bridge. "You'll have to strike a light. It's high up, to your right, of course, not very wide, looks like the result of a defect in the original form."

"We've got it." The Fed's voice boomed beneath the low arch. "The money?"

"No, not the money!" That was Sarcoff. He was on his way back. His foot slipped, and they could hear him curse and the splash of water. Sarcoff, right foot and ankle drenched, appeared at the mouth of the arch, an angry flush on his cheeks. "I don't know how they got it, but they got it, and the word 'Thanks' is chalked over the ledge along with their damned Greek letter!"

"The colossal brass of the blackguards!" Brun fumed.

"Chalked?" Cavanaugh said quietly, staring at Sarcoff's ruddy face. "You did say 'chalked' didn't you, Lieutenant?"

CHAPTER 17
THE BIG CRACK-OUT!

THERE WERE forty convicts under the watchful supervision of two guards in the prison yard during the afternoon exercise period. Lee Allyn, alias John Taber, kept somewhat apart from the others, the object of narrow-eyed, suspicious glances from a number of the other prisoners.

He might be able to fool the members of the Phi Gang, if it came to that, but the convicts who had known the real John Taber were already wise. Several minutes before, when they had lined up to go out into the yard, one of the prisoners had kicked Lee Allyn. It had been one of those close-in fouls, readily managed in a crowd; it might have passed as an accident except that Allyn had caught a glimpse of flickering hate in the other man's eyes.

They knew he wasn't John Taber, and the logical assumption was that Allyn was a police plant, a stool pigeon, smuggled into stir to spy on them.

Allyn had taken the foul in tight-lipped silence. There was nothing else to do. A brawl now, between himself and other prisoners, could upset the delicate mechanism which the Phi Gang had presumably arranged for John Taber's escape. So Allyn kept apart from the others, hoping that for the next few minutes he could avoid trouble.

His part in the getaway scheme, as intercepted by the Federal agents, was simple. He was to watch for an empty supply van which, by this time, ought to be somewhere within the gray walls of the penitentiary. The van would come along the concrete drive which bisected the prison yard on its way to the front gate. The back of the van would be open, the tail-gate hanging down.

Allyn was supposed to vault into the back of the van, flatten himself on the floor as close to the rear edge as possible, which meant he would be in full view of the guards and their automatic rifles. Beyond that, he knew nothing. Whether or not the guards had been taken into the confidence of the FBI agents, he didn't know, but he had been warned that there would be gunfire, plenty of it, and that it would be the real thing.

Allyn's gaze moved uneasily along the drive toward the gray walls of another building. The van would come from there, and he must not appear expectant. He glanced toward the huge iron gate, saw the guards that were posted just outside. Across the yard and close to the gate, he saw a little group of four men— he supposed you could call it a group though actually those four were not close together because of the watchful eyes of the guard.

Yet the four were distinct from the others in that they kept looking in Allyn's direction and then exchanging glances. In his nervousness, he interpreted their every gesture as a signal, a part of a silently planned move to mob him. One of the guards must have sensed something too, for he moved in closer to the four.

Behind the building at the rear of the yard, an engine was gunned. Allyn didn't look around, didn't trust himself to look. He could sense the slow approach of the heavy vehicle. He squatted on his heels, partially to appear unconcerned, partially because his knees had started to cave.

He picked up a piece of gravel from the prison yard, tossed it and caught it. A horn beeped a couple of times, and the prisoners grudgingly moved back from the drive, separating into two groups, one guard on either side.

The van rolled on. Out of the corners of his eyes, Allyn saw it. He caught and tossed the pebble once, tossed it again but this time did not catch it. He straightened onto caving knees, got a camera-shutter glimpse of the way the situation had stacked up.

The slow-rolling van was between Allyn and approximately half of the prisoners, and consequently one of the guards was concealed from his view. The other guard seemed to be chiefly concerned with the four trouble-makers who were considerably closer to the gate than Allyn.

HE SAW all this, and his mind goaded him into motion. This

was it—the split second of decision. And then as though in a dream he was sprinting the short distance to the rear of the van, he was vaulting lightly over the dangling end-gate and onto the van floor where he flattened himself full length on his belly and closed his eyes.

The van lurched forward. The heavy steel tail-gate swung upward and locked, closing the lower half of the opening, swallowing Allyn, providing protection against gunfire whenever it came. Why he had not drawn fire already, he didn't know.

He hadn't seen the thick snout of the silencer-equipped pistol that had pushed from a tiny port in the forward part of the van. For only a second the gun had showed, its single *plop* masked by the deep-throated roar of the engine, and the only guard who had been in a position to see Allyn's leap to the back of the van had been dropped by that shot.

But there were those who had seen the guard fall and who were always on the lookout for a once-in-a-lifetime break like that. At least a dozen prisoners fell in alongside of the truck as the iron gates swung open. They swarmed the gateman who immediately opened up with his rifle. He got two of the cons at close range before the others were upon him.

One got in a close-quarter kick, another wrested the rifle out of the man's hand and slammed the butt of it into his face. The con with the gun wheeled as the van pulled out of the drive, fired a shot at the guard on the opposite side of the drive. And the others poured through into the open, scattered widely, zig-zagged as they ran.

The alarm siren had started to scream. Guns from the guard

towers chattered. But the men were on the loose with two automatic rifles in their possession. Lee Allyn, in the back of the van, heard all of the sound and fury and supposed himself the object

"They call me 'The Chill.' Guess why."

of all the excitement. Yet not a single slug rattled off the armor plate of the tail-gate.

The van was now rolling at high speed, and as Allyn raised his head a little from the floor he noticed that the rear doors were swinging in to close off the upper part of the opening. The darkness was sudden and total. From somewhere forward, a man laughed.

"We'll never get a break like that again!"

The Senator stared in fascination at the gun in the man's hand.

175

"Four-twelve," another voice said. "And don't be so cocksure. This isn't over yet."

A steel door opened. The first voice said, "Hey, Taber, up on your feet and peel down to your underwear. Make it snappy. They may not sleep all day back there. Somebody must have seen you hitch this ride."

Allyn sat up on the floor of the van, unlaced the heavy prison shoes and got them off. He stripped out of the coarse gray shirt, lost a second patting his T-shirt to make sure that the footgear and contact lenses so vitally necessary to Captain Zero were still where he had hidden them. He stood, lurched to the wall of the van where he braced himself and got out of his trousers.

"All right," he called. "Now what?"

The second voice said, "Four-thirteen." Somebody acting as time-keeper.

The door in the false back of the van was opened again and a man stepped through carrying an electric lantern. He was a big man, broad through the shoulders, a wide face with widely-spaced, prominent blue eyes. He crouched beside the lantern, drew a pocket knife with which he slashed at the strings of large brown paper wrapped package.

"Get into these." He tossed a pair of women's shoes, each stuffed with a tan cotton stocking and a round rubber garter, to Lee Allyn.

"What the hell," Allyn said crabbedly. "I'm no sissy."

The other man laughed harshly. "Listen, pal, when orders from GHQ tell you to put something on, you put it on, see? Even if it's a wooden kimona, you put it on. Now get into them sausage casings, and don't worry too damn much about are your seams straight or not. You're going to be old enough not to care when we get through with you."

"Four-fourteen," the time-keeper sang out.

ALLYN SAT on the floor and pulled on the tan cotton stockings, the round garters, the low-heeled feminine oxfords. He heard the distant wail of a siren above the steady throb of the hard-pressed engine. The man with the broad shoulders kicked the paper package over to where Allyn was sitting.

"Get into your duds, grammaw. And don't forget the wig. It don't look like I'm going to be able to help you much. The prison screws finally woke up." He had moved forward in the truck cab, and now came back with a Tommy gun in his hands. He passed the spot where Allyn was struggling with the unfamiliar female attire, got to the rear of the van where he opened a slot for the gun barrel. The siren song was louder.

"You got your wig on backwards, grammaw. And button your dress, that ain't modest."

Allyn put his hands up to the gray wig and twisted it completely around. His fingers became ten thumbs when they got down to the small pearl buttons on the front of the yellow dress. There was still a coat and hat to add to his attire.

"Four-fourteen and forty-five seconds," the time-keeper called.

The man with the machine gun said, "I hope to hell it ain't a tie."

"What isn't?" Allyn asked as he stooped and picked up the shabby coat.

177

"A tie between us and the train," the man told him. "We're down to seconds now. We got to beat the limited across that grade crossing, see? That'll cut us off—*if* I can hold them off!" He broke off to fire a short burst from the machine gun. When he'd released the trigger, he said, "Ah!" with evident satisfaction. "I cut some rubber out from under them that time."

But there were other sirens behind them, and ahead Allyn could hear the *whoo-whoo* of a train whistle.

"Get this, grammaw," the machine gunner said rapidly. "If we make it across that railroad track, we ditch you on the other side. You go up through the cab and jump. There'll be cars lined up on the other side, waiting for the train to pass. Look for an old Dodge heading east."

"East?" Allyn echoed. "That's right back toward the prison, isn't it?"

"So what do you care? You're an old lady in the back seat of an old Dodge with another old lady. Under the wheel is a kind of greenhorn lookin' guy. And he's the boss from here on, see? You got nothin' to worry about except to follow instructions. You never was safer since you been out of your cradle."

The driver of the van tried for a final burst of speed. The vehicle trembled violently under the extra exertion from the hard-pressed engine. The train whistle was as a knife through Lee Allyn's eardrums. The van jounced, bounded, lurched across tracks, and Allyn fell flat onto his face in a world full of sound.

There was a gradual diminishing of noise, a steady deceleration until the van was moving at a crawl. The forward door opened and the voice of the time-keeper called:

"Let's go, Taber. But right now!"

Allyn scrambled up, but part of the yellow dress he had on didn't. A seam ripped, he didn't know just where and it didn't matter. He got through the door in the false wall, through into the cab of the truck where he crouched facing the open door.

"Old Dodge, remember?" somebody said. "We'll be abreast of it in a second. Jump, run behind the truck, and get into the back seat of the Dodge. *Now.*"

Then somebody boosted Allyn gently with the toe of a shoe. He jumped from the slow-moving van, managed to retain his footing in spite of the unfamiliar garments that seemed to have conspired to trip him. He glanced to the left, saw the train hurtling over the crossing.

There was a line of five cars on this side of the tracks, and the last was an old Dodge sedan, its driver a youngish man in a brown suit. In the back seat was a gray-haired old woman with a veiled face and a hat that was ornamented with large red cherries. One of her hands fluttered up, beckoning to him.

Allyn lifted the long yellow skirt of the dress and ran across the road to jump into the back seat of the sedan. He didn't say anything. His heart was way up in his throat and he probably couldn't have uttered a sound at that moment. The driver of the old car was looking at him in the rear view mirror.

The old woman beside him reached across, got hold of Allyn's skirt, and jerked it down over his bony knees. He glanced at her, at her profile, indistinct because of the veil. Yet that nose, that short, pert nose of hers—

She turned her head toward him suddenly. Through the veil,

their eyes met and locked. Her mouth opened as though to scream, closed as suddenly.

The two gray heads in the back seat jerked around to face the windshield. Lee Allyn and Doro Kelly stared straight ahead in silence.

CHAPTER 18
THE HOUSE OF DEAD FACES

"**G**OOD LORD, what are you doing here?" Lee Allyn whispered.

They had been traveling for hours—he didn't know how many hours—and now the old car had stopped at a filling station and the driver had gone to the men's room.

In the darkness, Doro Kelly's hand closed tightly on Allyn's. She said, "They think I'm Maria. Number Three, that is."

"And where the hell did they get that notion?" he asked acidly. "You didn't have anything to do with it, I don't suppose."

"A—a little," she admitted faintly.

"Well, now's your chance. Get out while the getting's good."

"I should say not!"

He turned in the seat and took the girl by the shoulders much as Captain Zero had done on the night before. "Doro," he said earnestly, "this is stark insanity. You can't get away with this."

"Maybe it is," she admitted, "but it's also sauce for the goose. Don't you see, one of us has a chance to pull through."

"Sure. I have," he argued. "This was all set up for me. You haven't got a snowball's chance in hell."

"Just as much as you have," she insisted. "That makes two chances to pull this thing off. The only way you'll get me out of this car is to throw me out. Try that and see what it gets both of us—a couple of slugs in our respective spines from that cannon Number Seven is packing."

He let go of her shoulders and sat straight on the cushions. He didn't know exactly where they were—some place north of Indianapolis, possibly. The station attendant had filled the tank, had finished wiping the windshield. He came to the back door of the car and said:

"That'll be two-eighty."

Doro said, "The Mister'll take care of it," in that cracked voice which she thought sounded like an eighty-year-old woman.

The attendant stuck his rag in his hip pocket and moved toward the door of the station. Following the man with his eyes, Lee Allyn noticed an electric clock in the window. The hands stood at 11:30.

"Hey, is that clock right?" he gasped.

She said, "I wouldn't know. I've been here so long I feel as though this seat and mine are practically the same thing. This is one time, Lee Allyn, when you're not going to get to bed on time."

He didn't say anything, but stared at the clock and took a brief glance at his own immediate future. If that clock was right, then in just thirty minutes from now he would begin to vanish. That Doro would discover that he was Captain Zero was the very least of it.

Number Seven would look into the back seat of the car and

discover that the old lady who was presumably John Taber had turned into a yellow dress and an old coat, a feathered hat with no face beneath it Number Seven would simply haul out his cannon and let Captain Zero have one right beneath the feather hat. Even if Zero managed to take out Number Seven before that critical moment, Zero would be just where he had been on the night before and the night before that—exactly nowhere.

HE STARED at the clock hands but he couldn't tell whether they had moved. He thought perhaps they had, and then again he thought maybe they hadn't. And now Number Seven came out of the men's room, walking deliberately. He paused, raised his left hand, and compared the watch on his wrist with the clock in the window.

"This clock isn't right, is it?" he said to the attendant as he paid the bill for gasoline.

The attendant chuckled. "Nope. That clock ain't run for six months now." He pulled out a thick nickel watch from his pants pocket, shook it, and held it to his ear. "I got five to eleven."

Number Seven nodded, strolled to the car, and got in under the steering wheel.

So that was the approximate time—five of eleven. Lee Allyn still had an hour before his invisible prototype took over. Which might be enough. On the other hand, they mightn't even be at their destination, wherever that was, by then.

The car started to roll again. When they had reached the outskirts of the little village, Number Seven spoke, but not to the two gray-wigged passengers in the back seat.

"Calling GHQ. Calling GHQ. Sector Officer Number Seven calling and standing by. Come in."

"You got a radio in this heap?" Allyn asked.

Doro forced a laugh. "They—we all have. All sector officers, anyway. Haven't you noticed the hearing aid Number Seven is wearing?"

Number Seven was transmitting again. "Position: Route 31, twenty miles north of Indianapolis. Everything under control. Awaiting orders. Come in, please."

In the darkness, Lee Allyn found Doro's hand and squeezed it. It was clear to him now how the Phi Gang had known that Captain Zero had been in the Oliver house the night that Mrs. Oliver had been murdered. And how they had known that Zero had hidden Mrs. Oliver in that closet.

Zero had knocked out the gang member who had entered by the front door, but the man's hearing-aid radio device had transmitted everything that Zero and Mrs. Oliver had said to listening ears of other criminals outside the house.

Number Seven said: "Taber, it looks like you're going to get a new face in a hurry."

"I—I am?" Allyn stammered. He noticed that since communicating with the gang headquarters by radio, the speed at which the car was traveling had increased.

"You don't sound too pleased," Number Seven called back, laughing.

"I always kind of liked my own."

"That's good, that is! Believe me after *I* cracked out of stir, I couldn't get a new face too fast to suit me. And if you don't get what I mean, you just shed that hat and wig and step out of this car in front of the first cop we come to. Maybe you don't know it, brother, but you're hotter than a little red firecracker!"

"You mean," Allyn asked, "that that pan you're wearing is something cut down and made over by a plastic surgeon?"

"Yeah. And you're on your way to the hospital for some alterations yourself."

So plastic surgery was the answer to the question as to why police had never recovered any of the criminals who had been liberated from prisons by the gang. Somewhere close to Indianapolis was a secret hospital where some renegade surgeon performed miracles under the direction of the master criminal. But unless Number Seven stepped on the gas Lee Allyn wouldn't have any face at all by the time they reached the secret hospital.

BESIDE HIM, Doro shifted her position restlessly. At her feet brown paper crackled. Allyn had noticed the shopping bag on the floor of the car and had wondered what it contained. Probably it was only part of the girl's disguise, he decided.

"Cigarettes, back there?" Number Seven was holding a pack over his shoulder while he drove. "No reason why you shouldn't smoke now, just as long as you don't set your wigs on fire. We'll be at the hospital in half an hour."

Allyn eagerly took one of the cigarettes.

"How about you, baby?" Number Seven invited Doro in that easy familiar tone which he had been using to address her ever since they had gotten out of the danger zone near the prison.

Doro took a cigarette, and Allyn asked where an old lady

was supposed to pack her matches. Doro's laugh was shrill, raw-edged. She pressed a paper book of matches in Lee Allyn's hand, too nervous, perhaps, to strike a light for herself. He held the match for her.

She had pushed up the veil and, in the flickering light, he examined her face. In spite of all she had done with the makeup, she couldn't make a hag of herself. She was still lovely, and how anyone could have possibly mistaken her for Maria Renard, he didn't know. Unless, of course, Number Seven had never seen Maria.

Allyn drew on the cigarette, settled back against the cushions and forced himself to relax. In half an hour, according to Number Seven's schedule, they would be at the secret hospital. And about twenty-five minutes after that, Lee Allyn would begin to disappear.

He wondered if it mightn't be wise if he slugged Number Seven at the first opportune moment and got himself and Doro out of this mess. They'd already penetrated two of the Phi Gang secrets—the plastic surgery angle and the means by which they kept in constant touch with one another. But was that enough?

Suppose they left it at that and Number Seven didn't turn up on schedule with his passengers. The master-mind behind the scheme would immediately smell a rat. He might scatter his forces, might move his headquarters to another part of the nation. And then the whole damn thing would start over again.

No, they had to stick. They had to stick with the thing until they knew everything. Or until they were—eliminated.

A shudder rippled across Allyn's shoulders.

"Look here, Seven," he said to the man behind the wheel, "it's swell to get out of stir and all that, but what does the gang want with me?"

Number Seven replied, "I wouldn't know, fella. Nobody knows but the Man in the Black Hat, and he never says any-things. Except 'Jump.' And when he says 'Jump,' you jump, see?"

Allyn said, "I don't like it."

"Why? What's the gripe? You're in the clear, the cops aren't going to touch you, and one of these days you'll have money to burn. Just string along with Black Hat, Taber, and I'm telling you, the sky is the limit."

Allyn smoked in silence and held Doro's hand. Just like a couple of babes, he thought, so deep in the woods they couldn't get out.

They were now passing suburban mansions near the north edge of the city, and Number Seven turned the car off the highway into a side road that climbed steadily and curved to the right. Then, slowing almost to a stop, they turned into a narrow, rutted lane where the headlights played on dense second growth timber on either side.

They were nearing their destination. After that—what? He couldn't even hazard a guess. Only one thing was for sure: twenty-five to thirty minutes from now and Lee Allyn would begin to fade out of the picture. If that happened under the watchful eyes of the Phi Gang they wouldn't wait until the transformation was complete. They'd kill him without any lost motion.

THEY CAME into a clearing, a large lawn choked with weeds. In the center of it stood a huge mid-Victorian house

186

of frame construction, painted a dull red shade. Every window from basement to attic was boarded and there was no sign of habitation. Number Seven parked the car in front of the rambling porch.

"Let's go," he said.

They climbed sagging steps. The front door was covered with boards and battens spiked into place, and Number Seven led the way past it to the side porch where he stamped on the floor boards three times, then stepped back quickly, bumping against Doro Kelly as he did so.

"Sorry, baby," he said.

A line of yellow light appeared at their feet, a crack in the floor that widened as a trap door creaked open. There were basement stairs that led down and through the foundation of the old house. They followed Number Seven into the cellar where doors opened on either side of a rock-walled passage.

And, oddly enough, one of the doors had a full length mirror. A voice that was nasal, metallic, and completely void of emotion spoke from a boxed-in loudspeaker above the mirrored door.

"Number Seven, you will send Taber to me."

Number Seven took Doro Kelly's arm. His cold eyes were on Lee Allyn's face. He jerked a thumb toward the mirror-paneled door.

"Go on in, Taber." And as Allyn hesitated, Seven looked at Doro and grinned. "We got things to do, haven't we, baby?"

Doro didn't say anything but clutched the paper shopping bag and moved off along the corridor with Number Seven. Allyn opened the door with the mirror in it and entered a small square room lighted by a naked bulb suspended from one of the floor rafters.

The room contained a folding chair and nothing else, the chair so placed as to face a second mirrored door on the opposite side of the room. If he had not known something about one-way mirrors, Allyn might have been tempted to snoop about the room, but he had a notion that his every movement was being observed by the Man in the Black Hat.

He went over to the folding chair and sat down, viewing his own ridiculous image with no enthusiasm whatever. He didn't know how long he sat there—too long, certainly, with the precious minutes ticking off toward the zero hours—before the metallic voice addressed him.

"You're no doubt glad to be here, Taber."

"Well," Allyn said dubiously, "yes and no."

"You enjoy prison life, is that it?" the voice asked sarcastically. "You didn't mind being deprived of the privilege of sailing your yacht?"

"Well, yes. I missed the boat like hell. What I meant was that my present situation doesn't seem to indicate that I'll be getting my sea legs back."

The voice chuckled. "Taber, how would you like to be admiral of the Atlantic Fleet?"

Allyn's heart skipped a beat and for a moment he could not shape any reply. His mind was busy with the component parts of the mystery. You had kidnaping, you had murder, and you had plastic surgery. You also had successful prison breaks.

Suppose that, through plastic surgery, it were possible to

substitute the most ruthless criminals alive for persons in high and responsible positions throughout the nation? Men like Burton Ivars who not only headed a large banking business but was being talked of as the logical selection for Secretary of the Treasury?

Suddenly, he knew why Sam Dawson had been so important to the Man in the Black Hat. Dawson was a master forger. If some renegade plastic surgeon could make over Dawson's face so that he would resemble that of Burton Ivars, there was no reason why Dawson couldn't be substituted for the kidnaped Ivars. Then if "Ivars" *did* get that cabinet post—

ALLYN WONDERED if he had successfully concealed his shudder from the eyes of the Man in the Black Hat.

"Well?" the voice reminded Allyn that he had a question to answer.

"I'd like it," Allyn replied. "Only I don't go in much for daydreaming, and I don't particularly like to be kidded."

The voice kept its silence for a time. Then, "Taber, you're not a common criminal. Not a professional, that is. You are simply a young man who, shall we say, borrowed a few hundred thousand dollars. Since you know nothing of crime apart from what you may have been able to pick up in prison, did it not seem strange to you that you should attract my attention?"

"Yes."

"You have been liberated," the voice continued, "because you possess a very special skill. You are an excellent navigator. More than that, you are a brilliant student of the subject of naval tactics. Is that not so?"

"Yes," Allyn said and prayed silently that Black Hat wouldn't start questioning him on any subject that had to do with the sea.

"It is this special skill of yours that I require," Black Hat informed him. "I have never discussed my long-range plans for the future with anyone, but inasmuch as I consider you somewhat above the common criminals with whom I usually work, I am going to give you a glimpse of what the future holds for you and for me—in fact, for all the loyal members of my organization. You will enter through the mirrored door which you are now facing."

Allyn got up and crossed the room. His hand on the knob betrayed his nervousness. He opened the door and stood on the threshold of darkness beyond which—even beyond the next room perhaps—he could hear muffled voices. There was at first nothing intelligible, and then one of the voices thundered out above the other.

"Fel-low Americans!"

"Aw, shut up, Senator! I'm getting damned sick and tired of that—" The second voice mumbled off into silence.

"Come in, come in, Taber," the metallic voice of the Man in the Black Hat spoke from near at hand. "And close the door behind you."

Allyn did as he was told mechanically, his mind numb from the shock of the half-revealed secrets and the incredible evil they portended. The only light within the room was that which screened through the one-way mirror glass in the door, and Allyn stepped aside to get full benefit of that.

HE SAW nothing except some dim, bulky articles of furniture that might be a desk. To his right and in front of him, he detected motion, a rustle of sound.

Then, on the opposite wall, draperies parted on a traverse rod like the curtain of a stage. He was looking through glass into the next room which was brilliantly lighted. There were three narrow beds, a number of chairs, two lamps, a console radio. There were two men in the room, one with his face swathed in white bandages. The other figure was striding back and forth in front of the beds, wearing pajamas and robe, gray hair rumpled above a florid face—a face Allyn had seen many times in papers and news reels.

Yet it was not, it could not be Senator Dunnwoody.

"You recognize the senator, no doubt," the voice of the master criminal said.

Allyn's glance jerked to the right. Within the room in which he now stood and to the extreme right of the glass panel, he could see a man standing in the shadows—a bulky, shapeless figure in some sort of coat with a turned up collar, wearing a wide-brimmed pork-pie hat. The Man in the Black Hat.

Allyn said, "That's not Dunnwoody. It can't be! The Senator is out in New Mexico. Why, I read in the paper—"

He broke off. What had he read in the paper? Yes. Of course. Senator Dunnwoody was missing.

Black Hat chuckled. "Yes, you read that the senator was lost in the Rockies, didn't you? I expect any moment now to receive word that one of my men has permanently eliminated Senator Dunnwoody. That man you see there will then be flown to the region in which the senator disappeared. He will be found, will go to Washington.

"And need I add that the bill providing for the creation of the Eastern Seaboard Power Commission will receive the approval of the Dunnwoody Committee and will be assured speedy passage? Need I also add that the good Senator will see to it that the power commission is headed by a man absolutely in my control? Step a bit closer to the glass, Taber, and notice what the man with the bandaged face is doing."

Allyn moved up to the glass. The man with the bandages on his face was sitting in a chair beneath the light from a bridge lamp. There was a clipboard covered with paper propped on his left thigh, and he was writing with a fountain pen. *Burton Ivars. Burton Ivars. Burton Ivars.* Over and over again the man wrote the signature of the famous banker.

"Does that mean anything to you, Taber?"

It meant a great deal. It meant that the kidnaped Ivars had been murdered, that plastic surgery would enable Sam Dawson to take Ivars' place.

Allyn said aloud, "It means you stand a fair chance of controlling the United States Treasury."

"Right!" the Man in the Black Hat said triumphantly. "All of the electrical power in seven Atlantic coast states. The United States Treasury. And, with your cooperation, Taber, I expect to eventually control the Atlantic fleet. What do you say now?"

Allyn took a shallow breath. "I know of only one thing that stands in your way. Just one person between you and eventual control of the entire nation."

"Yes? And who is that person?"

"The man known as Captain Zero."

Black Hat laughed harshly. "But, Taber, we *have* Captain Zero. He is securely locked in this building right now."

Allyn's trembling right hand lifted against the light that filtered through from the next room. He could clearly distinguish the bones of widespread fingers through the translucency of his flesh.

CHAPTER 19
UNDERCOVER AGENT

THE MOST difficult thing that Doro Kelly had ever done was to leave Lee Allyn in the basement corridor of the Phi Gang hideout. She had not been able to refrain from a final backward glance as his absurdly disguised figure disappeared from view.

Then she looked up into the cold, worldly eyes of the man known as Number Seven and tried to work up a smile. He didn't smile back and it seemed that his grip on her arm tightened.

"You and Taber got pretty well acquainted on that trip, didn't you?" he said sardonically.

Doro tossed her head. "There's no law against it, is there?"

Number Seven was leading her up a flight of concrete steps. "No, I guess not," he said flatly. "I'm surprised, that's all. From what I've heard about you, you're a pretty cold dish of fish and the exclusive property of Mr. Black Hat himself."

"Well, a girl can change her mind, can't she?"

For a moment he didn't say anything. Then he looked down at her and laughed. "Maybe you can change it again, huh, baby?"

They were at the top of the stairs, in semi-darkness. Number Seven suddenly caught Doro in his arms. His mouth smeared across hers and she twisted her head down away from his kisses. And then she brought a thick cuban heel down hard on Number Seven's instep. He threw her away from him, except for the hold he kept on one wrist. Even in the gloom she could see the hot brightness of his eyes.

"All right, baby," he said softly. "You want to play that way, it's all right with me."

He kicked a door open ahead of them, jerked her into what might once have been a kitchen. She dragged back, but she couldn't break that hold he had on her wrist.

"Wh-what are you going to do?" she gasped.

He looked at her. His smile was an effort.

"I'm sorry, baby, honest. Sorry about the kiss and the strong-arm stuff. Forget it, huh? I'm going to show you upstairs to a room. You can change into your own clothes, then I'll drive you to your apartment. After a little shut-eye maybe I'll look better to you, huh?"

She returned his smile that was an effort, too.

She allowed Number Seven to take her arm and lead her up a back stairway. Their footsteps echoed hollowly along the bare floor of a deserted corridor. Number Seven opened the door of a room and flipped on a light to reveal the meager furnishings—a bed, a chair, and a bureau.

A black, street-length dress, stockings, underclothing, platform sandals, a black cloth coat—all evidently Maria's—were laid out on the bed. At the sight of them Doro's heart leaped with renewed hope. The clothing held a promise of escape from this nightmare world in which she had lived for the past fourteen hours.

If she could play the game a little longer, if she could get Number Seven to let her out at Maria's apartment, then she could run to the nearest 'phone and call the police. She could direct a raiding party to this spot. Black Hat was here, the nucleus of the Phi Gang.

But what about Lee Allyn? How could she save him?

"I'll give you twenty minutes," Number Seven was saying to her.

"Yes," she said mechanically. She put the paper shopping bag down next to the door. She whipped up a strained smile for Number Seven who was backing into the hall and pulling the door shut after him.

Doro turned, started toward the bed, removing the cherry-festooned hat and gray wig as she did so.

TEN MINUTES later, dressed in Maria's clothes, she was peering into the bureau mirror and doing what she could about a face which had certainly begun to show the signs of strain. She paused in the act of applying lipstick and listened to the sound of the car that approached the house. Somebody stamped on the porch floor. Then there was silence.

Doro went on with her makeup job. She was rubbing a little color into her cheeks when the door of her room suddenly crashed open. She turned, startled. Number Seven stood there.

195

"Already?" she gasped.

Number Seven closed the door and leaned against it. His face was pale, his eyes narrow, "There's just one little detail we forget—you and I."

"Wh-what?" Whatever it was, she didn't think it was good—that one little detail they'd forgotten.

Number Seven stepped away from the door and came over toward her, like a panther moving on padded feet. "Why, baby, you didn't give me the sign. Remember?"

"The—the sign?"

Doro spun around. Number Seven stood there, holding an automatic on her.

"Yeah. How do I know you're really Number Three?"

Doro forced a laugh. "That's ridiculous. Of course I'm Number Three."

He nodded. "Okay, but how about giving with the sign? Just so we'll all be sure huh?"

"The sign," she muttered, staring at him as though she might be able to pick his mind that way—as she might pick a lock. She didn't know any sign, unless he meant the Greek letter *phi*. She hesitatingly raised her right hand, forefinger extended, drew a circle in the air and put a diagonal through it. She looked at him to see how that had gone over, and it hadn't gone over at all. She smiled faintly.

"Sometimes," she said, "we do it differently. Sometimes like this." She made a circle with the thumb and the forefinger of her left hand while the extended forefinger of her right formed the diagonal across it.

"We do, do we?" he said flatly. "Sometimes we do it like that, huh?" He laughed harshly and took a step toward her. "Now I'm going to tell you something, sweetheart. That don't mean a damned thing. Some goofy dame on a newspaper in Pendleville decided she'd call us the Phi Gang just because the boss let his pencil slip once when he was in a hurry to dish out an order. And you know who that goofy female reporter is?"

She knew. The goofy female reporter was standing there trembling in a pair of platform sandals that were much too large for her.

"And guess who just drove up in a car just now?" Seven was saying.

197

"M-Maria!" Doro gasped.

"Yeah. The real Number Three. Told me all about how you knocked her out. And guess what—*she* knows the sign, and *she's* got *long* black hair. And I'll tell you something else, sweetheart, you're Captain Zero's gal friend. *Aren't you?*"

Doro's lips stiffened. "Yes!"

He reached for her, and she dodged back. She cried, "Yes, I am, and if you touch me, he'll kill you. Zero will kill you!"

He caught her by the shoulders. She twisted away, tried to run, but his arms lashed about her from behind, pinning her arms to her sides, tightening until she couldn't breathe.

"Listen, sweetheart," he whispered in her ear, "I got *more* news for you. We've *got* your Captain Zero. We've had him for quite some time now. And you know something else? There's something kind of *wrong* with this Captain Zero. I'm going to take you to him now, baby. You'd like to see what's wrong with your boy friend, wouldn't you?"

He lifted her from the floor and swung her around, shoved her toward the door and out into the hall. Then along the hall to another door. He kicked that one open, released her then, gave her a push in the small of the back. She catapulted into the room. The high heels twisted under her and she fell face forward. The door slammed behind her. She heard the snick of the lock. Then there was silence.

She raised herself, and her eyes moved frantically about the bare room. She didn't see anybody.

"Zero," she whispered pleadingly. "Captain Zero!"

From the corner of the room came the sound of laughter. Wild, savage laughter.

CHAPTER 20
THE FINISHING TOUCHES

FOR A moment after Black Hat's triumphant announcement that the gang had already snared Captain Zero, Lee Allyn stopped breathing. But as there was no follow-up statement—Black Hat did not say that he knew it was Zero who was facing him—Allyn began to wonder if the Man in the Black Hat hadn't made one of his rare mistakes. Black Hat had, in Allyn's opinion, made two others already.

"And after we have complete control of the United States," Black Hat was saying as he pulled shut the drapes across the glass partition, "we shall set about controlling the rest of the world. Not a difficult task, my friend, considering the very jittery state of the world today."

In darkness that was total now except for the light that filtered in through the one-way mirror in the door, Allyn could hear Black Hat move across the room toward the desk. Allyn raised his right hand against the light from the door, and could see the apparently empty sleeve of the woman's coat he was wearing.

It had happened. The transformation had taken place, and Lee Allyn had become Captain Zero. But in the dark, Black Hat had no way of knowing it. Not yet, anyway.

"You could direct the action of the fleet against, say, New York harbor, Taber?" Black Hat's voice asked in the gloom.

"Yes," Allyn replied, trying vainly to keep the strange, resonant quality out of the voice that now belonged to Captain Zero. At the same time, his hands were busy. He had lifted the woman's hat he was wearing, had drawn the gray wig down over the invisible face of Captain Zero. Now he was parting the hair to make eye holes directly over his glasses.

On the desk in front of Black Hat, a ruby light glowed in the murky blackness, and Allyn saw a black gloved hand move to a switch and pick up a receiver. Black Hat had said he was momentarily expecting word that Senator Dunnwoody had been eliminated. Had the message come?

Black Hat listened in silence to the receiver, and then suddenly let the receiver drop with a clatter from his numbed hands.

"Taber!" he rasped out, "we've got a spy in our midst. It's that damned girl! The one that was with you and Seven."

Doro! They'd unmasked Doro.

"And what will you do?" The calm that Zero managed surprised even him.

"Do? Kill her, of course. She'll be eliminated immediately. Go on, Taber, get out of here. Dr. Kent will take care of you. I've already instructed him. Get out. I've got work to do. And I've got to do it fast."

Zero was already on his way to the mirror-paneled door. He pushed it open, crossed the lighted room outside, passed through another door, and into the stonewalled basement passageway. There was somebody waiting there for him—a tall, stooped man in a white tunic. Dr. Kent, no doubt.

200

The doctor opened his mouth to say something, left it sound-lessly open as he saw the face of the "woman" who was running toward him with her skirt above her knees. The face was covered with gray hair. If the renegade surgeon could have seen beneath that wig and observed the black space of Zero's face—he might have passed out cold.

Zero gave no warning. His invisible arms, covered by the long coat sleeve, reached out. His invisible fingers closed like steel talons on the throat of the medical man. Dr. Kent never uttered a sound, wouldn't have known what to say anyway. Zero tripped him, spilled him onto the floor, hung onto the man's throat in order to raise the head and bring it down sharply on the concrete. It was all very easy.

As Captain Zero, Lee Allyn was a different man from the reporter of the *World,* not at all averse to violence when necessity demanded it. It was as if a strange strength of purpose seized hold of him whenever he became the fabulous champion of justice—Captain Zero. Odd, he mused, that Lee Allyn in his daylight hours could never hope to put on a show like this one.

Dr. Kent was out cold. Zero straightened away, caught him by both arms and dragged him into the unlighted furnace room of the old house. Sleep tight, sawbones, Captain Zero thought. Pleasant nightmares. And you'll have 'em.

Now, Zero's mind hammered, to find Doro Kelly.

UPSTAIRS, IN the room into which Number Seven had thrown her, Doro got to her feet and staggered toward the corner from where that wild laughter had come. She had seen no one there yet, and for a moment she believed what Number Seven had told her—that the gang had Captain Zero trapped here and that there was something definitely wrong with him.

But now, as she rounded the foot of the bed, she could see a man lying on the floor in the corner. He was wearing brown pants, and a white shirt that was soiled and streaked with blood. His face was pillowed against his arm, and somewhere she had seen that light, very blond hair.

The man was breathing, sobbing quietly like a broken-hearted child. Doro put out a foot and touched him gently in the ribs. The man turned onto his back. His shirt was open, revealing his naked chest striped with long, raw, open cuts. Doro's indrawn breath was a scream in reverse as she recognized the round, boyish face, the feverish eyes of Arthur Henshaw. The wolf—minus his fangs.

He stared up at her. He laughed again, a crazy, shattered laugh, and Doro understood then those rips across Henshaw's chest. They had tortured him, cut into his flesh, lashed him with biting thongs.

"Go away," he said hoarsely. "Sure, I'm Captain Zero. I said I was, now go away. Don't hurt me any more."

They'd tortured him into confessing a lie—that he was Captain Zero. He'd told them he was to put an end to the treatment. And Doro understood how the Phi Gang might have assumed that Henshaw was Zero. On the previous night she and Zero had used Henshaw's car which had been parked for a while outside Maria Renard's apartment.

Doro crouched beside him. "Henshaw, listen to me. I'm not going to hurt you."

202

"I—I'm Captain Zero!" Henshaw turned onto his side, writhing away from her. He moaned. "Go—away. I said it, now go away. Don't hurt me anymore. Don't hurt me. I—I can't stand it. I can't—can't!"

Doro straightened helplessly, moved away slowly. Henshaw was utterly unable to understand anything. He was too maddened by the pain. Suppose they should try something like that with her to learn about Zero? Could she stand up under it?

She turned, ran to the door, seized the knob. The door was locked, solid as the wall. She ran to the window, snapped up the blind. Beyond was glass, and beyond the glass, thick wood planking nailed to the frame. There was no way out. She stood there, her chest burning, her heart pounding.

The sound of a key scraping in the lock brought her around to face the door, panic running through her. She stared wild-eyed as Number Seven reappeared, a heavy automatic pistol in his hand. There was no expression on his face now. He closed the door behind him, did not even bother to lock it. He indicated the gun in his hand.

"Too bad, baby," he said, but it was evident from his tone that it was not too bad at all. His eyes moved to the corner where Henshaw lay. "On your feet, Captain Zero."

Henshaw did not move. Seven's eyes were tight and hard. The line around his mouth deepened. He lifted the gun in his hand. The knuckles were white, every particle of his attention focused on the man in the corner. He did not see the door to the room behind him open.

Doro saw it. She did not look at it directly. She forced herself not to look at it, lest by so doing she tip off Number Seven. But she knew the door had opened—so quietly that Seven had not heard it. And then, while she stood there, too terrified to move, while the gun in Seven's hand steadied down on the form of Henshaw in the corner, Doro saw two guns in the room.

One was in Seven's hand, and the other, a small revolver that Doro recognized as her own, was floating magically in midair about four feet from the floor. And it was floating menacingly toward the exposed back of Number Seven.

"Get up!" snapped Number Seven. "Zero! I'll kill you!"

DORO WATCHED the suspended revolver in fascination. It rose slowly into the air, above Seven's head. Then it moved down with agonizing slowness. It seemed only to tap Number Seven on the right temple with its barrel.

Yet it must have been more than a tap. Number Seven started to fall, without a word, without a protest. That, too, was in slow motion. Seven folded up like a used sack of flour and collapsed on the floor. And then Doro was running across the room toward the spot where she knew Captain Zero was standing.

"Angel!" his deep gentle voice spoke to her. Doro sobbed as she felt his arms close about her. She shut her eyes. If I were blind, her mind told her, it would be like this. He would be to me as any other man. She kept her eyes closed, and his kiss was as any other kiss, yet sweeter and warmer than any she had ever known.

"So little time," Zero was muttering. *"We meet in danger and each tick of the clock tears us apart. We share an instant, and that instant brings us nearer violent death. Was there ever so strange a love as ours, angel?"*

She tried to answer, but he sealed her lips again with a gentle, firm kiss. She felt his unseen hands caress her hair, and then he tore himself away from her, almost as if he were breaking through chains to let her go. She stood with her eyes lowered, tears welling up in the corners.

His voice was choked and jagged and there was a bitterness in it that she had never heard before. *"So little time,"* he said again. *"Angel, Black Hat is going to move fast. We've got to stop him, or die. That hearing aid attached to the top coat of your shopping bag—"*

Doro was shaking her head. "It's a real hearing aid. It isn't one of their radios. But he—" she pointed to Seven—"he's wearing one."

"No. Get it," Zero ordered, his voice steady now. *"Get the real hearing aid. And hurry. You're all right. There's no one else on this floor."*

Doro got the hearing aid out of the shopping bag. When she returned, Zero had removed the radio device from Number Seven. Zero began to attach the real hearing aid to the front of Seven's coat.

"What's Henshaw doing here?"

"They think he's Zero," she replied. "The car, you know. We used his car."

"Yes, I know." His unseen hands were now fastening the receiver of the hearing aid to Seven's ear.

"And the sign," Doro said, "the one I thought was a Greek letter—it doesn't mean a thing."

"It meant something once," Zero contradicted her gently. *"The first time."*

"That was a slip," she said, her stubborn little nose going up in the air.

"*Yes. A disastrous one. Now tell me, angel, have you heard any of these radio messages?*"

Doro nodded. "I picked up an order from Mr. Big himself. There's some sort of an electric signal—"

"*We'll have to forget that. Maybe this one will be too groggy to worry about authenticity. Do you know his number?*"

"Seven," she said. "He's a Sector Officer like Maria. Mr. Big would say, 'Calling Number Seven. This is GHQ calling Sector Officer Seven. Come in.'"

"*You don't know where GHQ is, do you? That stands for General Headquarters.*"

Doro shook her head. "Maybe Seven knows."

"*I'm gambling everything on that. Watch him a moment. If he shows any signs of coming around, let me know.*"

ZERO CROSSED to the corner where Henshaw lay. A moment later, Henshaw appeared, unconscious, suspended in the air, arms dangling, heels dragging. Zero was pulling him across the room toward a closet. Doro hurried to open the door for him. Henshaw disappeared into the closet. And then the door closed, and the quiet, penetrating voice of Zero said:

"*There's only one way out, angel. You've got to go with Number Seven. I don't know how many of the gang are here—Black Hat—certainly, and the bogus senator, and Sam Dawson, alias Burton Ivars.*"

"And Maria."

"Yes, Maria. And you wouldn't have a chance of getting to that basement trap door alone."

She said stubbornly, "I'm not leaving you here alone."

"Yes you are. Pretend you're unconscious, and when Seven comes to, he'll carry you out of here on orders from GHQ. Only GHQ is me, for now. He'll have his gun, but watch this."

Seven's big automatic lifted from the floor. The clip pulled out from its butt, the cartridges quickly jumped out and went flying under the bed. The magazine rammed back into place, and the gun slid onto the floor within easy reach of Number Seven. Then a leather key container moved out of Seven's pocket. The key container sailed toward her and pressed itself into her hand.

"I'll have Seven put you in back of his car. You follow Seven and Maria to GHQ, wherever that is. Notify the police when you know where it is. Got it all?"

She nodded. "What are you going to do?"

"I've got to block the big pitch. Got to prevent Black Hat from pawning off his puppet as Senator Dunnwoody. Better get your revolver, angel, just in case. And make like you're old told. Our friend shows signs of reviving."

Number Seven had stirred slightly. She picked up her revolver from the floor, hiked up her skirt, slipped the gun under her garter, its muzzle in the top of her tight stocking. Then she got down on the floor, flat on her back, and closed her eyes.

"Not squinting like that," Zero warned her. *"Relax those eye lids."*

"I—I can't." Doro sat up suddenly. "Lee Allyn! He's around here somewhere. He may be in danger."

"I'll take care of him. Just lie down and relax. Everything will depend on you and me."

Zero moved to Number Seven. He got down onto his hands and knees beside the man, touched the switch on the hearing aid case. His heart was pounding madly. This *had* to work, and it had to work in time. There was no other way.

Calmly, quietly, his lips close to the tiny grill of the plastic hearing aid case, he started to speak. As well as he could, he imitated the metallic voice of the Man in the Black Hat.

"Calling Number Seven. Calling Number Seven. GHQ calling Seven. Come in."

Seven's eye lid fluttered open. He winced at the glare of the light, closed his eyes tightly again, and groaned.

"Calling Sector Officer Seven. Come in, Seven. GHQ calling Seven."

Seven rolled over onto his back.

"Calling Seven. This is GHQ calling Seven. Come in. Come in at once!"

Seven sat up so suddenly that he almost bumped Zero's invisible head. Seven clutched the edge of the bed for support.

"GHQ calling Seven," Zero whispered, counting on the amplifier within the hearing aid to build up volume in the receiver so that Seven wouldn't know the voice was coming from within a few inches of where he sat.

SEVEN REACHED up, fumbled the switch on the plastic case to off position. He said, "Hello GHQ. Hello GHQ. This is Seven. Go ahead, GHQ." He flipped the switch again.

"Hello, Seven," Zero said into the hearing aid mike. *"Zero*

at large. Zero at large." Seven turned his head sharply toward the corner where Henshaw had been. Perhaps in his mind he concluded that Henshaw had pulled a vanishing act and knocked him out.

"*Listen closely,*" Zero went on. "*These are your orders. You will carry the girl, Zero's aid, to your car. Put her in the rear seat. I will personally attend to her. You will contact Number Three. You and Number Three will go to GHQ and take over further transmission. You will call all Sector Officers and men to report in person at GHQ as soon as possible. All Sector Officers throughout the nation. Is that clear?*"

Seven flipped the switch, which simply turned off the hearing aid. "All clear," he said and moved the switch again.

"*Move at once,*" Zero ordered. "*I have no further communications as I will next contact you in person.*"

Seven turned the hearing aid off, got to his feet. He moved unsteadily to where Doro Kelly lay, crouched, got his hands in under the small of her back and her knees, lifted her limp figure. He stood there swaying, eyes squinted against the light. Then he lurched through the door, out into the hall, and down the front stairs.

Zero was only a few paces behind Number Seven and the precious burden that was Doro Kelly. Downstairs, in the front hall, Seven ran into Maria Renard looking somewhat more pale than usual. Maria frowned.

"What are you doing with her?"

Seven said, "She's going out. I'm to put in the back seat of my car and leave her for The Hat to handle. You know Zero is on the loose?"

"No!" Maria gasped.

"On the loose. And you and I are to get downtown to the garage. To take over the transmitter. Got to call in everybody for a council of war, or something. Give me a hand with this babe, can't you? She's not getting any lighter."

Maria took hold of Doro's ankles, and together they carried her through the hall into a huge living room. From there to the kitchen. Zero was right behind them, slipping through doors before Seven could close them, alert for any slip that Doro might make which would reveal that she was not actually unconscious.

Down in the basement, Maria, Seven and Doro climbed the steps to the trap door. Maria stamped on the fifth step from the top. The trap door slowly opened. They went through, but Zero remained at the foot of the steps, watching the trap door close.

He waited a moment, listening. He heard a car start, and then, only a few seconds later, a second engine kicked over. That meant that Doro was on her way, tailing Maria and Seven.

"Good luck, angel," Zero murmured and started along the passageway, the route he had taken when, as Lee Allyn, he had first been brought into the house.

Zero stepped to the mirror-paneled room. He pushed the door open. It was empty. He crossed to the mirror-paneled door, paused, listening for any sounds. Everywhere there was silence, and it struck him as peculiarly ominous. Suppose he was too late? Maybe they had gone.

HE PUSHED the mirrored door open, stepped into the blackness of The Black Hat's office.

"*Black Hat,*" he said softly.

There was no answer. He moved across the room to the drapes that concealed the one-way mirror glass panel. He parted them with his hand, looking into the lighted room beyond.

There was only one person in the next room. Sam Dawson, his face and head completely bandaged, sat in a chair. His pen and clip board with which he had been practicing Ivars' signature had fallen to the floor. His head had nodded forward, as if he were asleep, and from the bunched-up form of his suit coat, the butt of an automatic protruded. Sam Dawson, looking not at all the dangerous criminal he actually was. Asleep.

Zero let the curtain fall. He moved along the wall until his sensitive blind-man's fingers located a door in the end of the room. He tried the knob. Unlocked. Door opened, he stepped into the small operating room of Dr. Kent.

A door at the end of the operating room communicated with Dawson's bedroom. Zero's hand closed cautiously on the knob, turned it over, pushed the door open only far enough to slip through.

Dawson was snoring lustily. Zero moved toward him, stepped behind the chair. He looked down at the butt of the gun visible in the bulge of Dawson's coat. He steadied himself for a moment, then his right hand knifed down, caught and pulled out the gun.

Dawson was instantly awake, tipping forward in the chair, his bandaged head snapping around. He stared into the cold hollow eye of the suspended automatic. He sprang to his feet, staggered one step backward.

"*Hold it, Dawson!*" snapped Zero. "*You know who I am, and you know what I'll do to you—but with pleasure!*"

Dawson lifted his trembling hands shoulder high. "Yeah."

"*Where's Black Hat? Where's your pal, the Senator?*"

Dawson shook his head vigorously. "Not here. They just left."

"*Where, damn you? Talk, or I'll kill you! In a hurry!*" The gun floated around the chair and jammed hard in Sam Dawson's middle.

Dawson waved a hand vaguely. "Airport. They said something about an airport, a plane. That's all I know. I swear to God that's all!"

Zero caught Dawson by the shoulder and spun him around. He rammed Dawson's spine with the gun. "*Put your hands down at your sides and walk to the door. I'm right behind you.*"

Dawson moved to the door, opened it. They crossed the operating room, Black Hat's office, the reception room beyond, and then into the stone-walled passageway and to the foot of the steps.

"*Get that trap door open!*" Zero ordered. Wherever the airport was, it would not be far distant, for only two cars had left the hideout—Maria's and the old Dodge in which Doro Kelly was following. Unless, of course, Doro had failed.

They went up through the trap, onto the porch, around to the front of the house. The Dodge was gone. There were no other cars in sight.

"Around the house," Zero ordered, shoving Dawson ahead of him. *"How long since they left?"*

"J-just now," Dawson stammered. "Just a minute ago."

But Dawson had been asleep. It might be ten minutes, fifteen—long enough for them to reach a plane hidden nearby. Long enough to accomplish a getaway for the fake Senator.

At the back of the house bright moonlight showed Zero a path that wound through the trees. He goaded Dawson forward at a dog trot, and suddenly, through the crowded trees, he could see the firefly wink of some kind of light ahead in the distance. And just then an engine kicked over, sputtered, and roared into life.

AT THAT instant Dawson hurtled headfirst into the thick underbrush by the side of the path, hunching himself up into a knot, somersaulting over into the darkness. Zero could hear him crashing through the brush, but he could see nothing of the man.

In the distance the motor gained strength and was hitting hard on all cylinders. Zero glanced quickly at the pinpoint glimmer of light ahead, and then back into the thicket.

"Come on out, Dawson," he shouted, *"or I'll shoot you!"*

A low, sardonic voice came back from the blackness. "Come and get me, Zero. Come and get me!"

Zero's lips pressed into his teeth. *"I haven't got time for arguments, Dawson! I can see in the dark, and I'll kill you!"*

An echoing laugh was Dawson's answer, and with the sound of the laugh came a crashing of brush, a hurtling shape in the darkness, and the smashing weight of Dawson's body, flailing out blindly at Zero's invisible form.

Zero shot three times, reeling back from the screaming, bleeding man on top of him. Dawson's body hit the ground, twitched into a knot, unbent in the throes of death, and let go suddenly. Zero wiped the sweat from his invisible face, and ran on through the trees, a sickness and a nausea welling up inside him.

He was at the edge of the clearing and he could hear a voice. It was the bogus Senator. The voice carried across the flat space of ground. "What was that?" asked the Senator.

"A shot," Black Hat answered. "Seven eliminating Zero and the girl friend." That was followed by a metallic laugh from The Hat.

Zero had come to the edge of the clearing and now in the full moonlight he stepped out into the open. He could see The Hat and Senator Dunnwoody II starting off across the field to the shiny cabin plane that was warming up at the opposite side of the clearing.

"Hat!" cried Zero, letting his resonant, vibrant voice carry off across the cold air of the night.

The two men stopped dead in their tracks. Black Hat spun about, his eyes darting frantically about, probing the blackness of the woods. "Zero!" The Hat gasped, the words crawling up out of his throat. The Senator stood there, his eyes glassy with horror.

Zero waggled the heavy automatic so the moon's light glinted on the shiny barrel at all angles. *"Over here, Hat."*

Black Hat hunched over, grabbing for his shoulder gun. "Duck!" The Hat yelled to the Senator. "Flat!"

The Senator crouched and grabbed for his jacket pocket.

The Hat drew a gun swiftly and blasted away at the glint of Zero's automatic. Hot lead sizzled through the air around Zero's unseen face.

"Not quite accurate enough!" he yelled back, his voice mocking. *"Try again. Hat! And then if you've had enough, come on in under a big white flag!"*

FRANTICALLY THE BLACK HAT slammed more shots at the tree. Bark flew off into the blackness. The Senator blasted away at the invisible Zero, too, but the slugs found only bark and branches and tree trunks.

"Come on in, Hat!" yelled Zero. *"I'm giving both of you a chance. Come on in with your hands empty, both of you."*

The Senator jumped to his feet. "He hasn't got a gun, Hat! He's bluffing!" Throwing lead at the tree behind which Zero stood calmly—leveling the automatic at him—the Senator ran across the field, fully exposed in the moonlight.

"You damned fool!" cried Zero. *"Stop!"*

The Senator ran on at him. Zero could see his face now, clearly outlined in the light. His face tightening, his head throbbing, Zero brought the sights onto the Senator's upper body and fired a quick shot. The Senator went limp all at once, as if all the sand had run out of him, and he slid over headfirst onto the dirt, like a collapsing bird winged in flight.

"You fool! You damned fool!" Zero whispered, the futility and the uselessness of it all sweeping over him.

Two down—how many more to go?

"Throw down that gun, Hat!" Zero sang out, his voice steady and hard. *"Hear me?"*

215

The Black Hat was crawling over the terrain, hugging the ground, lining the sights of the gun again on the spot where Zero stood behind the tree. "You'll never get me alive, Zero!" snarled The Hat, blasting out another shot. "I've got these woods full of my men! They'll come at you any minute now! You want to wait?"

A lead slug tore off bark in front of Zero's face. Dust and splinters flew into his face.

Then, realizing it was no use reasoning with a complete madman, Captain Zero slowly lowered the gunsights on the slithering figure of The Black Hat as he crawled forward across the exposed terrain. Zero squeezed the trigger slowly, tightly, and the shot came and he could see the body of The Man in the Black Hat suddenly pitch over sideways, hover there an instant, suspended in air, as if it were undecided which way to fall. Then it slowly settled down into a crumpled heap.

Zero ran over to the spot where The Black Hat had fallen. The gun was lying harmlessly on the ground. The Black Hat's left trouser leg was sticky with blood. But he would go on living.

Until the big switch of the electric chair was closed, he would go on living.

With a curiously deadened interest, Captain Zero peered down into the face of the Man in the Black Hat. He stared at it a long time, and then he stood up again. At last he knew—for sure.

"He had everything," Zero muttered to himself. *"Why did he want so much more?"*

CHAPTER 21
LIKE DUCKS IN A TUB

" **T**HIS IS GHQ calling. GHQ calling all Sector Officers. Report here as soon as possible. All Sector Officers, wherever you are, report in person as soon as possible."

The voice of Number Seven was hoarse. After all, he had been
doing this for something over five hours now. They wouldn't let
him stop. They would let him have a drink of water once in a
while, and then Lieutenant Sarcoff of the Indianapolis police
would say:

"Okay, Barton, on with the broadcast. The show must go on,
you know. It's not over yet."

That was Seven's name—Barton. Bugs Barton, late of Alcatraz. They'd fingerprinted him, of course, as soon as they had
cornered him and Maria Renard in the radio room above the
parking garage in downtown Indianapolis.

And now he was on the air, just like Gabriel Heater or maybe
Bing Crosby, except that he wasn't getting paid for it. They—
Lieutenant Sarcoff and that wooden-Indian cop from Pendleville—wouldn't even suggest that Barton's sentence might be
lighter if he cooperated. It was cooperate, or else.

"GHQ calling all Sector Officers. Report in person as soon
as possible."

A plainclothesman opened the door of the office and stepped
in. Sarcoff stopped the broadcast momentarily by touching the
switch.

"How many now, Clancy?" he asked.

217

The plainclothesman smiled in evident satisfaction. "Seventeen so far. It's like shooting ducks in a tub. I guess after a few days of this and we'll clean them all up. They just drive in here with those hearing aid things on and we pick 'em up."

Cavanaugh stood up. He said to Sarcoff, "Okay if I get some breakfast for our mellow-voiced announcer here? He's going to need a barrel of coffee if he's got to keep that up all day."

"Sure, go ahead," Sarcoff said.

Cavanaugh sidled past the man in the doorway, went out into the room with its mirror-door. There he stopped, took off his hat and smiled as Doro Kelly and Lee Allyn entered.

"Is this where we audition, Mister, so we can get to be radio stars?" Doro asked.

Cavanaugh said gravely, "You're both stars in your own right already. Both you and Allyn."

Allyn smiled shyly. "I didn't do anything, except get in the way. It was Captain Zero." For Doro's benefit he had added that. He felt that she was still inclined to wonder why Lee Allyn always disappeared about the time Zero showed up.

Cavanaugh showed Doro to the door of the next room. "Go on in there and watch the broadcast. That's an old friend of yours at the mike, isn't it?"

When Doro had entered the radio room, Cavanaugh drew Allyn to one side and pumped the little man's hand for a long time.

"How many so far?" Allyn asked.

"Sixteen in the trap here. That's not counting Dr. Kent and Mr. Big himself and Maria Renard. They are all jugged. And

Dawson and the bogus Senator are in the morgue. But do you know, Allyn, I was right on Brun's trail immediately after the pick-up of the ransom money?

"He gave me the slip, of course, but at least I knew who we wanted. He got a little too smart for his britches when he ducked under that bridge to deposit the ransom money. He wrote 'Thanks' above the Phi Gang sign on the bridge, using chalk. Since the only conceivable approach to that bridge which a gang member could have made and not be seen would have been under water, I knew then that Brun was our man."

ALLYN NODDED. "I get you. The chalk would have dissolved in the water. What Brun actually did do was take the money down to the bridge, conceal it on his person, and then walk back while you and the rest of the cops hung around and tried to catch the criminals."

"That's it," Cavanaugh said. "So I followed Brun and lost him, as I said. Then I went to his home and checked on the pigeon business. The pigeons were in the loft of the carriage house. He was releasing them periodically by electrically controlled doors to their cages. They simply flew from the carriage house to the loft of the main building."

Allyn said, "He made another beaut of a mistake, now that I think about it. All of the ransom notes, though they were plenty brusque, addressed him as *Major* Brun. Yet he's practically the only person in the U.S. who still thinks of himself as an army officer. Did the tip about the oranges and the ranges help any?"

"It did," Cavanaugh said. "I printed '10ORANGES' on a piece of paper and put a diagonal through the second cypher, showed it to Sarcoff, and asked him if it said 'one hundred ranges' or 'ten oranges.' Sarcoff, who had served under Major Brun in the first World War, unhesitatingly decided in favor of the oranges. So that suggested Brun, too."

Allyn nodded. "I wasn't sure about that part of it. I'd heard somewhere that Army Intelligence uses a special alphabet for hand-lettering so that every possibility of misinterpretation is eliminated. The diagonal distinguishes the letter 'O' from a cipher, is that it?"

"That's right," Cavanaugh agreed. "Sarcoff told me all about it. And if Sarcoff had seen the newspaper with that on it, he'd have known that somebody with previous experience in military intelligence had written it. It was a slip on Brun's part. Presumably that was a last minute change in his plans, and he wrote the note in a hurry. The habit of putting the diagonal through the 'O' tripped him up."

"And as soon as he read in the paper the significance that the *World* had put on that mark," Allyn said, "he decided to adopt it as the signature of the gang to throw us all off the trail."

Doro Kelly came out of the radio room at that point. She looked smilingly from Allyn to Cavanaugh. "Which of you two nice boys is going to provide breakfast for a hungry girl?"

"I am," Cavanaugh and Allyn chorused. They looked at each other and laughed.

"I mean, we are," Cavanaugh said.